MORE PRAISE FOR BLOOD & CIRCUMSTANCE

"That such a slim volume can pack in so much depth
is a testament to the author's ability to spin layers of
meaning in deceptively simple prose, making *Blood and
Circumstance* a gem that should not be overlooked."
—Sarah Weinman, *The Baltimore Sun*

•

"Hollon is one of Alabama's best kept literary secrets...
six novels later, he continues to put his own singular spin
on the legacy left behind by his Southern forebears...
brilliantly compose[s] new lyrics for the old, dark songs
sung by those who came before him, Southern masters like
Robert Penn Warren and William Faulkner."
—*The Anniston Star*

•

"Hollon's skills as a storyteller and his experience as an
attorney give him a confident handle on his subject...
He has a talent for anticipating his audience's need...
his writing style is appealing, and his descriptions are
colorful and well-conceived."
—*Mobile Press-Register*

•

"An intense and satisfying read...What kind of author can
pack three novels into one? A damn good one!"
—Beth Goehring, *The Literary Guild*

MORE PRAISE FOR BLOOD & CIRCUMSTANCE

"…another mystery for the thinking person…
Hollon's a powerful writer…The unforeseen plot
moves will leave you with whiplash." —*Record-Courier*

•

"…spare and evocative prose…Though this novel
could be described as a legal thriller, the story is really
a psychological puzzle-box, filled with questions about
the nature of sanity, responsibility, justice, and mercy
in a world where there are no easy answers."
—*Mystery Scene Magazine*

•

"I'd recommend Hollon's *Blood and Circumstance* sooner than
one of Grisham's courtroom thrillers."
—*Birmingham Magazine*

OTHER BOOKS BY FRANK TURNER HOLLON

The Pains of April (1999)

The God File (2002)

A Thin Difference (2003)

Life Is a Strange Place (2003)

The Point of Fracture (2005)

Glitter Girl and the Crazy Cheese (2006)

blood and circumstance

a novel by Frank Turner Hollon

MACADAM CAGE

MacAdam/Cage
155 Sansome Street, Suite 550
San Francisco, CA 94104
Copyright © 2006 by Frank Turner Hollon
ALL RIGHTS RESERVED.

Library of Congress Cataloging-in-Publication Data
Hollon, Frank Turner, 1963-
  Blood and circumstance : a novel / by Frank Turner Hollon.
    p. cm.
  ISBN-13: 978-1-59692-196-2 (hardcover : alk. paper)
  ISBN-10: 1-59692-196-X (hardcover : alk. paper)
  1. Fratricide–Fiction. 2. Murderers–Fiction. 3.
Psychiatrists–Fiction. 4. Psychological fiction. I. Title.
  PS3608.O494B66 2006
  813'.6–dc22

                                                        2006019864

Paperback Edition: January, 2008
ISBN-10: 1-59692-267-2
ISBN-13: 978-1-59692-267-9

Manufactured in the United States of America
10 9 8 7 6 5 4 3 2 1

Book and jacket design by Dorothy Carico Smith.

For David and Sonny

I prefer winter and fall, when you feel the bone structure of the landscape—the loneliness of it—the dead feeling of winter. Something waits beneath it, the whole story doesn't show.

—Andrew Wyeth

He stands in the kitchen doorway, a black figure surrounded by the yellow light background, the small details of his face unseen from the darkness of the living room. His left shoulder leans slightly against the threshold, a pistol suspended from the left hand, dangling in the yellow space between the hip and the dark.

The other man sits on the brown couch in the living room, his face in one hand, crying. The sounds are muffled and light, but the anguish is deep and extreme. His breath catches in places along the line from oxygen to escape, and the body silently convulses with every catch. It is more than a bad day or even the death of a friend. It is the sight of life being gagged upon, forced upwards, and expelled into the cold air. The eyes tight-shut under the pressure of unclean fingers. The wetness and the dirt and the snot running slowly past the scars down the wrist to the elbow and soaking through a round point on the thigh of the jeans. The low smell of metal and medicine and the hum of the cylinder inside the shaved chest. A pistol in a cold hand resting in the lap.

The man in the doorway closes his eyes and remembers. The memories tell the story, and the story ends the same. There is no real purpose except the purpose we create. You make it or you don't, and if you don't, there's no reason to wait. No one's coming to the door to explain. It's like sitting in the waiting room of an abandoned building. Eventually, you have to get up and leave. Eventually, against all hope, you must recognize the futility.

His eyes open to see his brother on the couch, the muted light touching his shaking arm and shining on the clear liquid. He has shit his pants again, and the stench overlays all other smells and drifts without restraint through pockets of air to the four walls.

The step forward is deliberate. The futility recognized. The strong are always the chosen. "Why is that?" he thinks to himself. "Why are the strong always the chosen?"

"Because they choose themselves," he answers, five steps from the threshold, and two steps from his only brother.

And his brother looks up. And the pistol is raised, and the barrel points precisely, and there is the human hesitation, and then the pull of the trigger.

With the sound of the explosion in the cold room, misery ends, and yet for the living, only continues.

SESSION I
(Monday, January 17th)

I don't know much about the law. Believe it or not, my experience with the criminal justice system was limited. It's not limited anymore.

The sound of the gun was unbelievably loud. I just stood there with the noise vibrating inside my ears. Don't get me wrong, I didn't fail to grasp the weight of the moment, having just shot my little brother in the side of his head, but I'd already done all my crying beforehand. I'd already spent years and years agonizing over the decision. It was almost a relief, to get it behind me, to move to the next step in the process. I called the police, and now I'm right smack in the middle of the next step in the process. But this part never really mattered anyway.

My father was crazy as a fuckin' loon. Certified, honest-to-God crazy. I watched the mental illness eat away my brother, from the inside out. It was just a matter of time, and it's just a matter of time for me. You can't get away from your blood, and my blood's poison. I imagine tiny blue balls floating through the river of my veins, each filled with toxic liquid, the outer blue shells of jelly slowly melting away, releasing the poison into my blood until I end up just like the old man and Danny, rubbing my hands over my head and talkin' crap. You wonder, does it sneak up on you, slowly, until you don't know the difference, or does it hit quick out of the black, like a full punch in the face? I guess I'll find out soon enough.

Because mental illness runs in the family, and because they can't find a motive to satisfy themselves, and also because I won't let them argue self-defense, my two court-appointed lawyers decided to have me evaluated to determine my sanity at the time of the shooting, as well as my competence to stand trial. What do I care? Maybe the doctor can help me understand a few things I haven't figured out for myself. So I agreed to cooperate.

Before I met the doctor he had me take a bunch of written tests: Wechsler Adult Intelligence Scale, Wide Range Achievement Test, Bender-Gestalt, Multi-phasic Personality Inventory, and Competency to Stand Trial Assessment. It was like being in high school again. At first I thought I'd just blow it off and fill in the dots, but I figured, what the hell good would that do? The man's got a job, and besides, maybe I really am crazy. Maybe this is what it's like. After all, I'm sittin' in a jail cell for murdering my only brother, who I loved by the way, and I've got all these little tiny blue capsules floatin' inside me, each one about the size of a cricket's eye.

He was a tall, lanky guy, about six foot three, with glasses, maybe forty years old. Dr. Ellis Andrews introduced himself with a smile. We met in a conference room in the county jail, separated by wire mesh, but I could get a good look at him. He wore a wedding ring. It wasn't too shiny anymore so I figured he'd been married a good long time. There was a watch on his left wrist, one of those digital watches with a black rubber watchband. Some folks wear watches like jewelry, for decoration, intended to impress. Other folks, like Dr. Ellis Andrews, wear watches because they really like to know what time it is.

"Good morning."

"Good morning."

"How you feeling?"

"Pretty good, I guess."

He sat down and started shuffling through some papers. I saw the tests I'd taken days before. His face was a good face, clean shaven, solid, but not too hard. He wore a short-sleeved shirt, and I could see lots of dark hair on his arms, which was odd because he didn't strike me as a hairy man.

"Joel, you know what I'm here to do, and I know from your tests you're a smart man, so I won't talk down to you. I need you to be open and honest with me. Nothing you say in our conversations can be used against you. I'm here to learn about you and give the court an opinion on your mental state at the time of the incident and your competence now to stand trial. I'll put together a written report. The District Attorney, and your lawyer, and the judge, will all receive copies. Do you understand?"

"I understand."

"Are you willing to talk to me, answer my questions?"

"I'm ready. I've got nothin' left to hide. It's like water built up behind a dam. Get it started and gravity will take care of the rest."

I've always had really good eyes. I can see things other people can't. Dr. Andrews jotted a few notes on a yellow pad. Upside down, through the wire mesh, in his scribble, I could make out most of his words, but I didn't let him notice me looking. I figured it might come in handy.

"I hope those tests turned out alright. When I got arrested, they wouldn't let me get my glasses. It was a little blurry."

"I can help you with that. Just let me know who to call."

"It's O.K., I'll get my mom to bring them up next time she comes."

He wrote down, "Subject appears late twenties, white male, five feet ten, 170 pounds, brown hair, blue eyes. Strong eye contact. Intelligence test reveals high IQ. Education level high school graduate, one year college. No obvious indication in written tests of malingering or deception."

"How old are you?"

"Twenty-eight. No, I'm sorry, twenty-nine. It's strange to forget how old you are. It seemed so important when I was a kid."

"I guess we'll just start at the beginning, Joel. What's the first thing you remember?"

"Ever?"

"Yes. The first thing you remember as a child?"

"Well, I've got some early memories, bits and pieces, you know, like my mother's face, but I guess my first complete vivid memory is when my father wrecked the truck down the road. He was a crazy son-of-a-bitch, you know? I mean really. Screwed-up-in-the-head crazy. But how can you know that when you're a little kid?

"I was about five, I guess. Danny was just a baby. My dad was off somewhere, and he called home. I could hear him screamin' through the phone at my mother. That crazy screamin'. The kind my mother couldn't control.

"You gotta understand. We lived underneath the man everyday. It was like a hurricane sittin' off the coast. You got no way to know what it might do. And I guess she loved him like a person might love a hurricane. It's necessary. You might as well love the fuckin' thing, even if it doesn't know.

"Anyway, he was screamin' through the phone. Somethin' about the dog. Somethin' about me not cleanin' up the dog shit in the backyard. And for some reason, he took the dog with him that day. He told my mother he was comin' home to beat my ass, and she was tryin' like she always did to calm him down. It was nighttime, and rainin' outside, and he said he was comin' home to teach me a lesson about bein' a man in this world."

"Was there mental illness in your family?"

"Yeah. I was told my grandfather died in an institution somewhere, but I never met the man. He died before I was born, which is O.K. with me."

"Go ahead."

"Anyway, Mom hung up the phone and tried to tell me not to worry. But I knew different already. I knew what he could do. I'd seen it.

"We waited. I sat at the front window and waited for the headlights of the truck. But they didn't come. I remember hoping he'd gone off again like he sometimes did. Gone off to wherever he'd go for days at a time.

"And then the phone rang again. I remember the sound made us both jump. My mother was afraid to answer the phone, but she did anyway, and I could tell somethin' happened. My father wrecked the truck just down the road from the house. A neighbor lady called.

"I remember wishin' he was dead. At five years old, I didn't know what dead really meant, but I remember closing my eyes and wishin' he was dead. Think of that.

"The dog didn't even have a name."

"What happened?"

"We went out in the rain to see, me and Mom and Danny. She had him wrapped up in a blanket with his head covered. She got an old umbrella. I was in my pajamas. I remember they were blue. The kind with feet. Mom made me put on my little boots. I guess she figured I was safer with her than back at the house alone. In case the crazy son-of-a-bitch walked away from the wreck and came to the house through the woods or something.

"We could see the headlights of the truck up against a pine tree. The neighbor lady was out in her yard. As we got closer, I could hear the windshield wipers on the truck still slapping back and forth. There was no ambulance or cop cars there yet.

"My momma made me stand back a few yards. She put down the umbrella and opened the truck door real slow. The inside light came on, and I could see my father slumped over the steering wheel. A whiskey bottle fell out on the grass at my mother's feet. When I think about it now, I wonder what she was feeling. I wonder if she was hoping he was dead, too. Or if she was worried about the son-of-a-bitch, like you might be worried about a wild animal caught in a trap.

"Anyway, he wasn't dead. He started to moan a little bit. The window on the passenger side was either rolled down or busted out. I kept standin' on my tiptoes in those little boots, tryin' to get a look past my father to see the dog. But the dog wasn't there. He was gone. I ran around the other side of the truck in the mud to look for him. I remember callin' for the dog, lookin' out in the black woods for any movement.

"The ambulance showed up. My momma had the neighbor lady take me and Danny inside her house. It smelled like mothballs. Our house always smelled like my father. I watched through the window as they put him in the ambulance, and I cried for the dog. The dog with no name. Maybe I was cryin' because the old man wasn't dead. I don't know. I just remember thinkin' about that black-and-white dog somewhere in the dark woods, alone, afraid, not understanding what happened, or what was gonna happen next.

"You know what I mean?"

"Was your father's mental illness ever diagnosed?"

"I don't know. I doubt it. I'm not exactly sure what that means anyway. If nobody gives it a name, can we pretend it didn't exist? Does the illness make the diagnosis, or does the diagnosis make the illness?"

"Do you mind if I talk with your mother? Maybe she can provide some family history and background."

I was careful with the question. I didn't want to appear hesitant, but I hated the idea of my mother going through everything again. I glanced down at the doctor's notepad. I couldn't make out the first sentence. The second line said, "Possible manipulation."

"Yeah, you can talk to my mom, but be nice please. She's been through enough."

I closed my eyes and felt emotion come up inside. I could have cried, but I didn't want to.

"Are you alright?"

"Yeah, I'm O.K."

"Tell me more about your father."

"He was a tall man, skinny, like you. My brother favored him. I look more like my mom. Maybe that's why the old man was always harder on me than Danny. Or maybe he just knew I could take it.

"I don't want it to sound like the old man was always a bad father. There were times, when he took his medicine and stayed away from the bottle, he could be a good father. He was a funny old bastard. Always tellin' stories. He had a quick mind when his mind was right, but mostly I remember the times when we were scared of him.

"He smelled weird. It's embarrassing when you're a kid and your friends say your dad smells weird. He let his fingernails and toenails get long and yellow. Mom would have to sit him down and cut his toenails like he was a baby. She was always on his ass to take his pills, cut his toenails, take a shower. She'd hide the whiskey and some nights you could hear the crazy bastard going room to room looking for his whiskey bottle.

"He talked to God."

"What do you mean?"

"He used to tell us God would say things to him, and he would say things back. When I was a little kid he told us God ordered him to plant twenty-seven Christmas trees. So he did. Twenty-seven Christmas trees in a row along the back of our property. He said God told him he would be alive twenty-seven more years, and so he would need twenty-seven Christmas trees.

"Every year after Thanksgiving he'd go out with his saw and cut down the next tree in line. We started out with little trees, just little scrawny trees in the living room with a few Christmas ornaments hanging off like earrings on a skinny street whore.

"He died on the fourteenth tree. I guess he wasn't talkin' to God after all. The other thirteen trees are still lined up in the backyard. They're big now."

"Do you believe in God?"

"That's a pretty big question. Does the definition of insanity include belief in God?"

"Let me ask the questions, please."

"I mean, my daddy believed in God. He believed he had conversations with God. And I know my daddy was insane. If I say, 'Yes, I believe in God,' does that put a check in one of your boxes? What if I say, 'No, I don't believe in God? Maybe the men who wrote the Bible were like Thomas Jefferson and Benjamin Franklin, they wrote the Bible like those guys wrote the Constitution. As the population grew to unmanageable numbers, somebody had to make the rules. Somebody had to lay the groundwork for a civilized world. So they came up with the ten commandments so we wouldn't kill each other, or steal from each other, or fuck each other's wives. They came up with heaven and hell, a reward for doing right, a punishment for doing wrong. They used the fear of eternal damnation as a tool, because nobody could prove they were wrong. Man's natural fear of the unknown, life after death.'

"Don't get me wrong. It's a brilliant concept, the idea Jesus may show up tomorrow so you better do right today. And you better be nice to everybody because that guy you cuss or kick when he's down, that could be Jesus himself. Your judge and jury, right there in the flesh.

"No, Doc, at the risk of sounding perfectly sane, no, I don't believe in God, at least not the God who told my daddy to plant twenty-seven Christmas trees in a row behind our house."

My voice had risen, and I could feel the skin on my forehead tighten like a rubber band around my skull. The doctor was taking notes, but I wasn't looking. He seemed ready to change the subject, and so he did.

"How did your father die?"

"I was twenty-one years old. I'd been staying at the house, mostly because I was afraid to leave my mother and little sister there alone with him. Danny was in and out of the crazy house, and dad was mean as shit. He was a man of extremes.

"I remember the day before he died like it was this morning. He was thin and old like a skeleton, but that mean bastard could lock his hands on you like he had metal fingers. We got in a full-blown fight."

I had gone over that day in my head a thousand times, at least, but saying the words out loud to the doctor was different. I had never lined up the words in sentences to make sense to someone else. It took me a few seconds to put together the idea.

"What was the fight about?"

"This girl died in our front yard. She was a teenager out driving around one night like teenagers do, and she flipped her car on the curve. It killed her. The car landed on the edge of our front yard at two o'clock in the morning. They carried her away in an ambulance, but she was already dead.

"About a week later, on a Sunday morning, I was sitting at the kitchen table drinking a cup of coffee. I saw the girl's momma drive up and park on the road. She got out in her Sunday dress and put a little wooden white cross in the grass where her daughter died. I watched her dig up some dirt and plant little pink flowers at the base of the small cross.

"She was on her knees. From where I sat I could see tears rolling down her face. The girl's name was written on the cross. Jenny was her name, in little black letters on the white cross.

"I watched the lady lift herself up from the ground

and wipe the dirt off her hands. She stood back from the cross, and I'm sure her mind wouldn't let her stop seeing her baby coming around the curve that night, and the car flipping, and her daughter lying dead in the broken glass, her eyes closed. The lady finally left.

"A few hours later I heard my father go outside. He walked to the little cross with the flowers and stood there. I wish I could know what he was thinking. I wish I could know.

"He walked around the back of the house, and I heard the riding lawnmower start. I stood at the front window, the same window where I sat that night waiting for him to come home and kick my ass. I watched my father drive the lawnmower across the lawn and over the white cross. I watched the wood pieces spit from the blades and the pink flowers scatter in the air.

"What kind of motherfucker does such a thing as that? You tell me, what kind of motherfucker runs over a dead girl's cross with a lawnmower?"

I felt my blood pressure go up. It was like I was there all over again. Right there, at the window, watching that motherfucker do what he did. I looked up at the doctor, and he was looking at me real close, like he was seeing something worth writing about.

"What happened?"

"I went out in the yard and yanked him off the lawn-mower. I think I would have killed him if my mother wasn't there."

"That was the day before he died?"

"Actually he died that night, in his sleep. Real peaceful-like. The doctor said he died around eleven o'clock that night, but my momma didn't notice a thing until the next morning when he wouldn't wake up.

"She slept in the bed all night with a dead man, just a few feet away, in the bed with her. It was probably the best night's sleep she ever had."

"Were you sad when he died?"

"Sad? I'm not sure what sad is. I was glad he wasn't in the house anymore. I was glad my mother didn't have to worry about what he might do the next minute. I wish he had just gone off in the woods and died like an old dog instead of dying in my mom's bed, on her clean sheets.

"You know what? We buried him at night. We had a night funeral, almost like my momma thought she could sneak the sorry bastard into heaven when nobody was lookin'. Maybe God wouldn't notice until Daddy was already in the door.

"Let me ask you a question. You do this for a living, study folks. How do you separate pure meanness from mental illness? My daddy was mean. He mighta been crazy, but he was mean underneath. Danny was different. He suffered, but he didn't hurt other people. At least not on purpose.

"How do you separate those things?"

"Sometimes you can't, Joel. Mental illness affects all kinds of people, nice and not so nice. Sometimes symptoms of mental illness can be violent outbursts or episodes of uncontrolled anger, but it's not really possible to blame everything your father did on his mental problems."

Dr. Ellis Andrews looked like a big bird. I could tell he wanted to take a peek at his watch, but he didn't want me to see him look. At least he had enough respect not to appear bored while I spilled my guts.

I didn't care what time it was. In jail, who gives a shit if it's 10:35 or 2:35? There's nowhere to be. Nobody's waitin' at the movie theater or the mall for me to show up. Even when I was out of jail, time didn't matter much to me. The division of days is completely manmade, an artificial separation. In reality, it's truly a flow of days like a river, one part inseparable from the next. You can't break it up for organizational purposes any more than you could divide the oceans into small square cubes and space them out neatly in the atmosphere.

None of it matters anyway. None of any of this matters at all. Dr. Ellis Andrews. His evaluation. My dead father. The tiny blue capsules floating, or not floating, as the case may be, inside my body. It just doesn't make any difference at all. The world spun around just fine before I was here, and I'm sure it'll keep spinning after they bury me in the dirt. There's nothing I can do or say one way or the other that makes any difference.

A high school teacher once told me about the stars. He said most of the stars we see at night burned out hundreds of years ago. "How's that possible?" I said. "I can see them, right up there in the sky."

"You can't see the stars," he said. "You can only see the light that left them hundreds of years ago."

He explained, "The light travels at 186,000 miles every second of every minute of every hour of every day. It's like a flashlight in the heavens suddenly switched off. The beam of light keeps traveling through space at 186,000 miles per second. That's how far away those stars were," he said. "That's how bright they once shined. All you're seeing is the light that left the flashlight a long, long time ago."

If that powerful star doesn't matter, how could a person really matter? How many people leave their light behind, hundreds or thousands of years after they've burned out? None, if you ask me.

I hate to think about the stars. When your father was

a lunatic, and you watched your brother go crazy in front of your eyes, and you're just waitin' for the next shoe to drop, crazy-ass ideas like the star thing can't stand alone. Any odd thought, any strange fear, can be the beginning of the slow, or not so slow, slide into dementia. You can't just take the idea for what it is. You have to wonder if it's the final weird idea that may take you over the line. The line you won't ever get back across, or maybe ever recognize again.

Still, the star thing freaks me out.

I said, "My dad used to tell my friends in the neighborhood he was a cheese salesman. He thought it was the funniest damn thing he ever heard. He told them the car trunk was full of cheese, different kinds of cheese, American, cheddar, mozzarella. And he said he drove around all day, door to door, selling cheese to folks. Big blocks of cheese.

"At first some of the guys believed him, but after he told the stupid story fifty times, they'd look over at me not knowing what to say.

"And the story always ended the same. He'd say, 'And we've got a special today on Swiss cheese. I won't charge you for the holes.'"

"What did your father do for a living?"

"There was a time he worked framing houses, but for

the last years he just stayed home and cashed his crazy check from the government. When folks get something for nothing too long, it changes 'em. You know what I mean? It realigns their DNA. They're not good for much after that."

"Tell me about your mother."

"Do you have to go somewhere?"

"No."

"Why you keep lookin' at your watch?"

"I didn't notice. I'm sorry."

Dr. Andrews hadn't actually looked at his watch, but now he wasn't sure whether he had or not. I rubbed my forehead and took a glance at his notes. "Positive eye contact except when speaking directly about his father. Quick to anger."

"Quick to anger," I thought. He ain't never seen "quick to anger." Then again, maybe he has. Maybe he's seen people in this very room rip off their own heads and flail about like the headless horseman, flinging blood in circles around the cream-colored cinder block walls. Maybe it happens everyday.

I looked him straight in the eye and said, "My mother is a good woman. Probably the best person I've ever known. And no, I never wanted to fuck her, if that's what you're gonna ask me next."

We stared at each other a few moments. We both waited patiently.

"Do you have a sister?"

"I do. I never wanted to fuck her either."

"Joel, do you want to end this session? I can come back later."

I looked down at my feet and pretended to feel bad for the way I'd acted. Actually, I didn't have to pretend.

"I'm sorry. Can I ask you a question?"

"Yes."

"Is the definition of insanity a person's inability to weigh the consequences of their actions, or is it the ability to weigh the consequences, but the inability to make the proper choice regardless?"

Dr. Andrews smiled. It was the first time I'd broken through. I had to pull him somehow outside the standard professional groove, outside the typical psychiatric trench warfare and into the open space of human communication.

"That's a heck of a question, Joel."

He wanted to answer, I could tell. There was a mind in there after all, buried underneath the Wechsler Adult Intelligence Scale, and all that bullshit education. I bet he'd be just as freaked out by the star thing as me, he just wouldn't admit it. To admit it would be to recognize the total futility of the next question. And to recognize the total futility would make him dead inside, just like me. Who's better off?

"My sister was our only hope. She was a lot younger, the furthest away from the old man somehow. I remember when she was little, her arms were always open. Me and Mom, and even Danny sometimes, tried to build a wall around her. Some nights I slept on the floor in front of her bedroom door."

"Where is she now?"

"I haven't seen her in a long time. She just left. She moved as far away from us as she could get, like the distance could lessen her chance of being like us. Like she could outrun her own blood. But you can't outrun it, can you? It's inside. It goes wherever we go. The old man lies beside us all.

"Her name is Lisa. I miss her, a lot."

"Does she know about Danny?"

"Above Lisa's bed my mother used to have a dreamcatcher. That's what they call it, a dreamcatcher. It hangs above a kid's bed, a blue crystal ball held in a copper wire circle.

"My mother said it would keep away the bad dreams

and hold onto the good dreams, but really, it was my mother who was the dreamcatcher.

"She would take turns sleeping in our beds at night. I wished it was my night every night, but being the oldest, there was a part of me that was willing to skip my nights so Mom could be with Danny or Lisa."

"Do you resent Lisa for leaving you behind to deal with the family problems?"

I thought to myself, "That was pretty good. He's gettin' down to the meat of the matter now."

"Do I resent her?" I asked.

"Yes. Your sister ran away from the problems. You chose to stay behind. Do you have any resentment about your sister or your decision?"

"It doesn't matter. It never mattered, and it never will. In fact, nothing in this world matters at all. Not one bit."

We were at a standstill. The doctor shifted up in his chair closer to me. He pulled the eyeglasses from his face.

"If nothing matters, Joel, then why did you stay behind to protect your sister and your mother? Why did you stay to take care of Danny? If nothing in this world makes any difference, why did you try to make a difference?"

"Because I didn't know better."

He leaned back in his chair and slowly placed the

glasses back on his face. There was a chip in the glass on the edge of the left lens. I wondered how long the man had neglected to replace the lens. I wondered if he sometimes saw a flash of rainbow light in the bottom of his field of vision. An illusion of light that wasn't really there. Maybe it appeared in front of the yellow paper as he wrote. Maybe he liked it.

"Have you ever been diagnosed with a mental illness, Joel?"

I laughed. "Yeah, lots of times. We didn't have insurance or money to see the right doctors, so Mom would take us to state doctors, or whoever the hell would see us. I remember first hearing the word 'schizophrenia' when I was about five years old. Maybe they were talking about the old man. I just remember hearing the word."

I laughed again.

"What's funny?"

"I just thought about why my mom took me to the doctor that first time. My father whipped the fire outta me one morning. I don't remember why. I just remember what I did to get him back.

"I was afraid of him then, but not too afraid to do what I did. He went off to work, I guess. My mother tried to make everything alright. She fixed me chocolate milk and let me watch TV, but I couldn't stop thinking about the son-of-a-bitch. It was just eatin' me up.

"I went to the bathroom and took a shit in the toilet. My mother was busy in the kitchen. I picked up the little log of crap and wrapped it in toilet paper. I snuck to my parents' bedroom. I pulled back the covers and wiped the crap on the mattress under my daddy's pillow. I rubbed it in hard, washed my hands, and then put the sheet and the covers back where they were."

"What happened?"

I smiled and shook my head. "Daddy came home that night. He didn't apologize, and I was glad he didn't because I'd already put shit in his bed.

"I just remember laying awake that night, waiting. I heard the old man yell, 'What's that goddamn smell?'

"I don't know if he figured it out, or if Mom cleaned it up or what, but the next day she took me to see this doctor who asked me a lot of questions. He had me do things with blocks and circles. I think he's dead now, the doctor.

"It wasn't until a lot later I got medication, which is a big trick anyway, isn't it?"

"What do you mean?"

"Medicine is supposed to make you well. You take medicine when you get the flu or chickenpox or whatever. It makes you well, and so you stop taking the medicine.

"I must've had the same conversation with Danny a thousand times. The medicine would make him feel good, good enough to stop taking the medicine, and so he'd stop. And the same shit would start all over again. The next thing you know he'd be running down the street naked.

"One night I got a call from the cops. They found Danny walking down the side of the road at three o'clock in the morning, completely naked. Not a stitch of clothes on him.

"Cop said he pulled his car over and Danny froze perfectly still, like a statue. Cop said, 'What the hell you doing?' Danny just stayed frozen. Cop said again, 'What the hell you doing?' And you know what Danny said?

"Danny asked, 'You can see me?'

"Can you believe that? He thought he was invisible. He thought if he took off all his clothes, nobody could see him. He was late coming home. He'd been drinking. So in his mind the safest way to get home without getting caught was to take off all his clothes: socks, shoes, underwear. Put everything in a pile under a tree. And then walk naked two miles back home.

"When I came to get him at the jail, the first thing he asked was, 'Can you see me?'"

"Did the medicine ever seem to help you?"

"No, it never did. It seemed to help my father and Danny, when they would take it, but I never got much good from it. Of course, I never thought I was invisible either.

"For some stupid reason I always thought they were giving me sugar pills. Even so, I felt like I could think clearer without it.

"It was different for Danny, though. He believed they were experimenting on his brain. He said the medicine messed up his seasons. He said he had seasons inside him: spring, summer, fall, and winter. They came and went at their own pace, always in the same order. It was the winter he couldn't remember. He said he would go to sleep one night in October and wake up somewhere strange, not knowing how he got there.

"That never happened to me. Not like that anyhow."

Somebody yelled out down the hall, "Get your fuckin' hands off me." The words vibrated down the hallway, and Dr. Andrews looked up over the top of his glasses at me. I think he wanted to see my reaction, the way a scientist might look for a reaction from a monkey who hears the cry of another monkey being tortured in the room next door.

He lowered his eyes and pulled out what looked like a page of form questions from inside his stack of stuff.

"Do you remember having any separation anxiety as a

child when you were away from your mother?"

"Do you have certain questions you always have to ask in these things?"

"Yes, Joel, I do."

"Who made them up?"

Dr. Andrews didn't answer.

"I mean who made up the questions? Do you think the guy who made up the questions is smarter than you?"

"Maybe, Joel. Maybe not, but it would be helpful if you'd answer this question and then we could move along to one you like better."

"I don't really dislike the question. I was just wondering. Anyway, yes, I remember having separation anxiety. When she dropped me off on the first day of school, in the first grade, I thought it was the last time I would ever see her. In fact, every single day, for my entire life, when I've left my mother's presence, I've imagined it would be the last time I would ever see her.

"You've got to understand. We didn't just depend on her for food and tucking us in at night. We believed she was the only thing that kept us alive, literally, everyday.

"I didn't say one word, not a single word to anybody, my entire first-grade year. I heard the teacher tell another teacher she thought I was retarded. That's a hell of a thing to say in front of a six-year-old. I wrote down on a piece of paper, in very correct penmanship, 'You are the retarded one,' and left it on her desk. Fat bitch."

"Did your mother teach you to read and write?"

"She did. She loved books. I guess they were her only escape. She would read out loud to us. I remember she used to take us to this secret place and read to me and Danny. She called it her church in the pines. It was a spot in the woods where eight or ten pine trees had grown twice the size of all the trees around them, tall with big round trunks. They were all bunched together. It was quieter than any place I've ever been. The sunlight would slice through in columns, yellow like butter. We would move our hands slowly though the beams of light from one side to the other.

"I wish I could go there right now. I would take you with me if you wanted to go, and show you the columns of light. If we could, if things were different, do you think you'd want to go?"

Dr. Andrews hesitated, and then nodded his head up and down slowly.

"Yes, I would want to go."

He looked down at the form questions and asked, "Have you ever had any physical problems, such as asthma, allergies, diabetes, seizures, or headaches?"

"No."

"Did you ever get hurt seriously? Trauma to the head, broken bones?"

"When I was eight years old I fell out of a tree down the street from our house. I hit my head on a root. It knocked me out pretty good.

"A man in the neighborhood, a preacher-man, found me and carried me in his house. He had a wife and two girls. One of the girls was in my class at school.

"You know, it's been a long time since I thought about it, but there was a feeling in that house. Different from my house. There was a gentleness. He carried me inside and laid me down on the couch. They put a cool rag on my head, and the lady gave me a glass of orange Kool-Aid. I remember it was orange. They were like a real family. It was calm inside that house. Maybe I was just delirious."

"Did you go to the hospital?"

"The man drove me to a doctor. I think he paid for everything. My arm was broken. They put it in a cast.

"One day, maybe a year later, the girl didn't come to school. They told us her daddy had a heart attack and died at his church. He was pretty young to die. The lady took her girls and moved away. I never could figure out why they lived on our street anyway. They just didn't seem to belong there.

"It's funny how we think the things we remember are somehow more important than the things we don't. I hadn't thought about that day in a long time. It could have been gone out of mind forever, like so many other things. And once it's gone, it's like it never happened."

"Have you ever been arrested before?"

"Yeah, nothing big though. Nothing like Danny. He got arrested enough for all of us."

"Tell me about your arrests."

"Well, I went a year to college. It didn't work out too good, but that's another story. There was a bar down the road from the apartment I was staying in. All you can drink for five dollars from nine to eleven on Wednesday nights. If you want to, you can drink a hell of a lot in two hours for five dollars. We were shootin' pool one night, and my buddies ended up leavin' me. I guess I decided to walk home around midnight.

"I walked down the railroad tracks alongside the street. The bar was about a mile from home. Don't ask me why, but for some stupid drunk-ass reason I decided to climb inside a coal car to take a piss. You ever been inside an empty coal car?"

"No, I can't say I have."

"Well, first of all, the sides at each end are slanted like

ramps. It rained that night earlier. I slid down the ramp easy enough to get inside, took a piss, and got ready to climb out.

"Well, there ain't no ladder to climb out. The sides that aren't slanted are too high for a normal drunk human being to jump up and pull himself out. I tried runnin' up the ramps, but every time I slid back down on my belly. It was dark, so I couldn't see I was covered in black soot from fallin' down and rollin' around in the mess.

"Pretty soon I was too tired and too drunk to have any chance of gettin' out of that hell hole. I was probably soaked in my own piss puddle.

"It sounds funny now, but at the time it didn't seem too damn funny, in the middle of the night, full of cheap whiskey, cold, wet with piss, black as a Sunday mornin' nigger.

"Anyhow, I just started yellin' and pounding on the sides of the coal car. Somebody must have called the cops. They got a kick outta the whole deal. I got arrested for public intoxication. Spent the night on the floor at the city jail because they didn't want me sleepin' in their clean beds."

I laughed and shook my head. Dr. Andrews held back a smile. I was curious what his laugh would sound like. Would it be short and squeaky, the way some folks laugh? A cackle? Or would it be a deep belly laugh, the kind that makes everybody else want to laugh along at the same time?

He just kept jotting notes on a yellow pad. "Minor criminal history. Alcohol. Verify through NCIC records to determine truthfulness. Subject has habit of biting finger-nails."

"Were you arrested any other times?"

"Just once, when I was a teenager. I let a monkey out of his cage at the zoo. I was there with a school class, a field trip I guess. There was this one monkey, a little brown one, in a big cage with maybe ten other monkeys. He just kept staring at me. Just me, like I was his only hope in the whole wide world. Like I was the only one who understood.

"When the class left the monkey area, I went back by myself. I stood there a long time, me and that monkey just lookin' at each other. Finally, I walked around the cage until I found a place where they fixed a hole with chicken wire. I pulled it loose until the hole was open.

"But you know what? That little monkey just sat there. He wouldn't move, afraid to be free. Afraid to move a muscle. One of the other monkeys found the hole and got loose. Somebody must've seen me do it, because I got in all sorts of shit over it. I'm not sure I was actually offi-cially arrested, but they took me down to the police station. They called my father.

"I sat on a bench in the police station and waited for my father to come get me. I sat there for hours, just waitin' to get my ass beat by the old man. But you know what? He didn't do anything. We just rode home in the truck, neither of us said a word. We went inside the house, and I could almost feel the belt leather on my ass, but he didn't do anything. He didn't say a word about it."

"I noticed earlier you used a racial term to describe black people. Do you have negative feelings toward black people?"

"No. I didn't mean anything by it. It was just a saying. I've tried awfully hard not to be like my father, and my father was a man who hated black people, and Mexicans, and most anybody else not like himself. He blamed them for everything he didn't have. They took all the good jobs, he said. They got special treatment. Jews ran the government. Mexicans were taking over America.

"My mother couldn't stand it. I heard the old man tell her he didn't have time to get to know people one by one. So if he didn't have the time, he had to bunch all of them together. Every black person was like the worst black person he knew. Every Jew, or every Mexican, or every Catholic, were like the worst ones he ever met or heard about on TV. I guess it's some kind of natural survival instinct. An animal must be able to recognize another animal immediately as a threat or as no threat. My father believed everybody was a threat, one way or the other.

"Being lazy is an evil thing. It breeds hatred. My momma taught me to respect everybody until they prove, one by one, they don't deserve respect. Not the other way around."

"Have you had any suicidal or homicidal thoughts?"

"Well, I suppose I've had homicidal thoughts. I shot my brother in the fuckin' head, didn't I?"

"Besides your brother, have you ever wanted to kill anyone else?"

"Well, hell yeah. I wanted to kill my dad a thousand times. I even thought it through a few times, from start to finish. From cracking him in the back of the skull with a baseball bat to burying his sorry ass in the backyard. But I never did it. I probably should have, but I never did."

"Why not?"

"Now there's a question worth asking. I bet that question isn't on the standard form. I bet some guy sittin' behind a desk in a Yankee university never thought of that question."

"Do you have an answer?"

"No, I don't, but I'm sure my inability to answer that question probably says more about me than any bullshit answer I could think up."

"What about suicide? Do you ever think about suicide?"

"Something's the matter with a man who doesn't think about suicide, a man who fails to figure out control of his own life belongs only to him. You have to find the courage to explore the darkness in your heart. If you can't find the courage, you can't really know yourself, or anyone else for that matter.

"Anybody who says they don't think of suicide is either a liar or an idiot. It's the only real choice a man makes in his entire life, all the other choices are diluted, watered-down selections of one worn path over the other."

We sat quiet for nearly a minute. Dr. Andrews wrote notes I couldn't see. The pad was tilted as he leaned back in his chair. He was left-handed. The long, thin fingers seemed awkward wrapped around the blue ink pen. In the relative silence I could hear the sound the pen made on the page, a soft scratchy sound, words from the mind of the doctor, in reaction to my words, traveling down the long, hairy arm to the hand, and from the hand to the pen, and from the pen to the paper, and later from the paper to some typed report of the analysis of my existence. It suddenly seemed so arbitrary and ridiculous.

Different words, different doctor, different-colored pen, maybe a different result. Maybe undo what I'd done. But I wouldn't undo it anyway, no more than I would choose to forget.

"I think we're done for the day, Joel. I'll be back on Thursday for our next session."

"What's today?"

"Monday."

He gathered up the papers in a brown binder. I watched Dr. Andrews rise from the chair, even taller than I first thought, and walk to the door behind him. His pants were baggy in the back; corduroy pants, believe it or not. The brown leather belt snaked around his waist, skipping the belt loop on his right hip. The door opened and then closed. I knew the door on my side was locked, so I just sat still in the little room, alone.

I closed my eyes and hoped no one would come for me, at least for a few minutes. I saw myself climb inside my mother's car, with Danny in the car seat in the back, and we drove down Highway 49 to the place in the woods, my mother's secret place, the church in the pines. We walked down a dirt path past a cotton field in full white bloom, like a sea of bright snow, hazy in the breeze. We walked in the woods a short distance, Danny in my mother's arms, to the spot where the big pine trees stood like ancient fingers reaching to the sky. I wrapped my arms around the biggest trunk, unable to reach even halfway, with the smell of pine sap close to my nose.

My mother opened a book, *To Kill a Mockingbird,* and read to us the stories of Scout and Jem. Her voice was soft and easy, and Danny just stared at momma's face, listening to the flow of the words, the rhythm of one sentence to the next. And around the words there was a silence, a gentleness like the gentleness in the preacherman's house, a calm before the winter. A sense of life with meaning.

I lifted my hand and moved it slowly through the column of yellow sunlight, feeling the warmth, watching the shiny specks of dust floating in and out of the column of light, and wondering.

I heard the clang of the keys on the metal door, and the turn of the lock, and the swing of the heavy door, and the touch on my shoulder.

"Get your fuckin' hands off me," I said.

SESSION II
(Thursday, January 20th)

The guard walked me down the long hall to the interview room. He unlocked the door and pointed inside. The room was empty, and I sat down alone, waiting. I hate the shoes they give you in jail. Plastic orange slippers, ugly and hard. Just imagine how many disgusting nasty-ass toes have wedged themselves up inside that shoe before it gets to you. Big meaty toes, hard yellow-brown toenails, flaky red fungus, curled-up smelly mutated puppet toes.

Dr. Andrews opened the door on the other side of the dividing screen. He was wearing the same shoes as before, brown lace-up leather shoes with a rubber sole. He carried the same ragged binder with papers sticking out one end.

"Good morning, Joel."

"Good morning."

He sat down across from me. On the left side of the

doctor's chin was a tiny piece of toilet paper with a red dot in the center. He must have cut himself shaving, put a piece of toilet paper on the cut, and forgot about it. Maybe he didn't care, but probably he was the type of man who would prefer I told him about it.

There was more gray in his hair than I noticed before, mostly around the temples. His glasses were just a little crooked, but not off center by much. Dr. Andrews opened the brown binder in front of him and shuffled through pages of notes. There was a manila file with my name on the top, Joel Stabler. He had a different ink pen, still blue, but fatter.

"Where were we?"

"You were asking about the time I was raped by my babysitter."

He stopped and peered over the top of his glasses. I let him swim in the ridiculous possibility he'd forgotten about something so important, and then I smiled.

"O.K., I think we were talking about your family."

"It all goes back to the family, doesn't it? I mean, it's the endless process of separating blood and circumstance to figure out who we are. It can't really be done, can it?"

"Not completely, no. But we can make some progress. Tell me more about your mother."

"She could make a hell of a cookie."

"What kind?"

"Sugar. She's kind of like a sugar cookie herself. Her goodness is pure. Simple and pure.

"She used to clean houses. She would take me and Danny with her to these big houses owned by rich people. We couldn't touch anything. It always made me feel sad to see her cleaning up those places, when I knew she deserved to have a home like that herself.

"She cleaned churches, too. This one church I remember the most. I told you about the preacher-man down the street. It was his church. Big and quiet on a Saturday night. I would sit with Danny on one of the long, brown, wooden pews, afraid to make a sound. We could hear Mom in the back with her mop and bucket. She gave us pencils and paper to keep us busy.

"One night, the preacher-man walked into the church while me and Danny were sitting there. He went up on the stage and stood in the pulpit wearing his robe. He saw us out there, a big, empty, echoing church with two little scared boys sitting in a middle row.

"And you know what he did? He gave his whole Sunday morning sermon. He gave the whole sermon, practicing for the big show the next day. And the entire time he spoke, he looked directly at us. I don't remember a single word, at least not how we think of words. I just remember the feeling. Like he was God up there, and we were under his eye and hand. Like we were completely safe from everything bad, but at the same time we couldn't move a muscle, or whisper a sound, without being seen or heard.

"His voice was loud, but calm, and I saw my mom standing at the doorway to the back room, watching the preacher-man, knowing she had to clean the toilets where the church people shit. She had to pick up their pubic hairs, and dig out the crap in the drains in their sinks. Pick up their cigarette butts one by one."

"Did that make you angry?"

"Not at the time."

"Does it make you angry now?"

"Yeah. A lot of things make me angry now."

The doctor's pen touched the paper. "Overwhelming sense of protection for mother. Prevailing hostility toward symbols of organized religion."

"Did you know your grandparents?"

"The only one was my mother's mother. We called her Joyce. She wouldn't let us call her any nicknames like other grandmothers. Just Joyce, which was kinda weird. But she was nice to us.

"My mother would take us to Joyce's house when things at home got really bad. She didn't like to do it. Sometimes we would sleep in the car, but if we had to stay away more than one night, momma would take us to Joyce's house. She kept a shotgun in the closet. If my dad had come to her house, even once, I think Joyce would have killed him dead. I think she hoped he would come over, just that one time.

"He never did."

"I didn't get a chance to talk to your mother since our last meeting. I'll go see her this weekend. What about your sister?"

"What about her?"

"Do you mind if I call her?"

"I don't know where she is."

"What's the age difference between you and your sister?"

"I was twelve when she was born. Danny was eight."

"Did you help take care of her when she was little?"

"Not really. My job was to stay between her and my father. She was so little and innocent. Lisa was hope."

"What do you mean?"

"Well, when she was born, it was like all our hope—mine, Mom's, Danny's—went into her body. Danny was already showing signs. Mom had given up on herself a long time ago. She lived for us, not for herself. And I knew my job. My job was to take the fist. Every time the son-of-a-bitch hit me, it was one less blow my mother took. That was the way it was.

"And by the way, I know you're the doctor, but you can't really have any fuckin' idea what it was like. You can sit there and take your notes, you can study the test results, but you can't really know anything.

"You ever see your mother vomit blood because your father punched her in the stomach so hard it lifted her body off the ground? No.

"You ever learn to sleep so lightly at night you could hear the bed squeak in the middle of the night in your parents' bedroom? So you could scramble out of bed to see where the old man was going? What room he was going to next? No. I can't sleep now. He's been dead for years, and I can hear a dog bark five blocks away and I'm sittin' up. You don't know what that is, or what it was like in my house, or anybody else's house for that matter.

"I took Danny into my own hands. My hands. I did what had to be done, and I'll be judged by people who cannot possibly know. Lawyers, a doctor, a judge, twelve strangers, who don't know me, or Danny, or anything about us. The further I go, the more fucked-up this gets."

My head felt hot. For a few seconds I didn't know where I was. It was a lightness. I took a few deep breaths and looked up at the tiny piece of tissue on the man's chin. It just hung there, held by the spot of dried blood. How could he not know? How could his notes and papers be so disorganized? They should be in order, each in its proper place, fitting together perfectly like bricks in a wall.

"Do you need a minute?"

"No, I don't need a minute. I don't need anything."

"Did you ever try to get away?"

"Sometimes when people leave, it's worse than dying for the folks they leave behind. We don't usually choose to die. But we sure as hell choose to leave. My sister left, and even though I was glad to see her get away, she took all of our hope with her, and it never came back.

"Let me ask you a question."

"O.K."

"Have you ever heard of anybody having little blue jelly balls in their blood system? They're very small, maybe the size of a white grain of sand, but they're blue and filled with poison jelly, like a bath bead, and when they break, the blue jelly gets out into your blood, and eventually into your head, mostly in the top part of the head. Right up here."

I touched the top part of my head where I felt the poison would float. The doctor wore a white, button-down, short-sleeved shirt. There was a small stain near the top button, reddish in color. I saw a scar I hadn't seen before, just above the top button, at the base of the neck. It was a half-inch long with dots on each side from the stitches laced long ago.

"I don't think I've heard of anything like that before, Joel."

"I figured you hadn't. I was just wondering. You know, I can still see Lisa, clear as day, sitting up in her bed in the morning, maybe two or three years old, looking through her books and talking to herself.

"She would be the first to wake up, and I would always hear her. She pretended to read the words she didn't understand, she only knew they made us speak sounds, and so she would speak the words she knew. The words that went with the pictures.

"I would sneak to her bedroom door and watch. Her hair was very blonde. The little fingers would turn the pages, and she would change her face with the expression. A sad face, and then a smile, and then very serious.

"We would sneak a cookie sometimes before anyone else woke up. A sugar cookie. They were good. Really good. And I can see her smile, and the dimple in her little cheek, and the fingers holding that cookie.

"'You weet, Joel,' she would say. She left the *s* off sweet. Sometimes we would sneak one of the old man's Cokes. I knew it was bad for her, having cookies and Coke for breakfast, but it felt too good to make her happy, even just for a few minutes before the possibility of a new day.

"The Coke would burn on the way down. Her little blue eyes would water."

"Did your father ever abuse Lisa?"

"No.

"A few years ago I tried to find her, but I couldn't. I traveled around for a while, just drove out west: Arizona, Colorado, California. There's a power that exists in lone-liness. It's hard to define, but you can feel it.

"Have you ever read *Catcher in the Rye*? That's the way I felt the entire time I was on the road. It's a strange feeling, having nowhere to go, hollow, with no real connection to the people you see everyday.

"Eventually, I had to come back home. I don't know how people can live that way for very long. I don't know how Lisa could do it. Maybe, on purpose, we kept her one step removed from the family. Maybe she found a place she belongs. I hope she ends up with a house full of her own kids. I hope they eat sugar cookies and drink cold Cokes everyday.

"Where'd you get that scar on your neck?"

Dr. Andrews lifted his hand to his collar and felt the scar with his fingers. He seemed to be surprised it was visible.

"It happened when I was a kid. Me and my brother were having sword fights. I guess I lost."

"You've got a brother?"

"Yes."

"Older or younger?"

"Younger."

"Is it cold outside?"

"What?"

"Is it cold outside? You've got short sleeves in January. I was just wondering if it was cold."

"Not really. I left my jacket in the car. You've got long sleeves. Are you cold?"

"Yeah, but I always loved the winter, gray skies. My mom hated it. She stayed cold all the time. I like the idea of everything dying and making room for everything new. You know what I mean? So much possibility.

"Have I ever told you what my mom looks like? She's a small woman, thin. Too thin. But she wasn't always that way. I've seen pictures of her. She was a beautiful girl. Brown hair, and deep brown eyes. Not hazel, deep brown. Her face is pretty, like Lisa's.

"And she was strong. I don't mean just emotionally, dealing with everything she dealt with in this world, but strong. I was always amazed how hard she could work, with a baby on one hip, pushing a vacuum cleaner across some rich woman's oriental rug. She never seemed to get tired, or at least she never let us see it.

"She looks tired now. She came to see me last week, and for the first time she looked tired. She's alone. Joyce is dead, Daddy's dead, Danny's dead, Lisa's gone, and I'm in jail.

"As hard as she tried to make everything O.K., this is how it worked out. Some decisions can't be undone. When you lie down with the devil, you wake up with him the next morning. That's just the way it is."

I stood up from my chair and walked to the far wall. No windows. I slipped off the ugly orange slippers and felt the coolness from the painted gray floor on the bottoms of my feet. I leaned my back against the wall and tried to feel the January air on the other side, tried to feel the grayness of winter morning.

Give me the sky first, and I'll work my way downward. I have the need to measure my world. I know where it begins, at the core of the earth. I just don't know where it ends. Give me the sky first, and I'll work my way downward. It's so much easier to measure that way. People say, "The sky's the limit." That's not true. The sky isn't the limit. It's just the beginning. It's just the edge of infinity.

"Do you think you're smart, Joel?"

"If I'm smart, I'm smart enough to know it. If I'm not so smart, then I'm stupid enough to think I am anyway. You can't learn anything from my answer to that question.

"Besides, what's the difference between smart and mentally ill? Not much. Men are not created equal. We might be equal in the eyes of your God, or even in the eyes of the law, in its purest form, but in reality, we aren't equal. Nobody's equal to anybody.

"I can't dunk a basketball on a ten-foot goal. I'll never be able to do it, no matter how much I practice, no matter how hard I try. The retarded kid in cell block #4 can dunk a basketball like there was nothing to it, but you know what, he can't keep a job at McDonald's, and he never will. And you know why? Because he's stupid. That's why he stabbed the kid who lived next door thirty-seven times. Because the kid next door called him stupid.

"You figure it out.

"Did you know there are people who believe extreme intelligence is a form of mental illness? They say Albert

Einstein painted his front door of his home bright red so he could find his house on the block. I heard he wore each pair of underwear exactly nine days in a row. That doesn't seem normal, does it?"

"How did you do in school?"

"As good as I wanted to, basically. I spent a year going to the community college. My father told me everyday it was a waste of time. I was surprised, but even my mother seemed against the idea. Maybe she couldn't get past her jealousy that she never had the chance to go, I don't know.

"I felt lost there. Like I didn't belong. One time I went to an English professor's office. In a huge bookshelf, all across the wall, he had first edition novels. Faulkner, Walker Percy, Robert Penn Warren. I lifted my hand to pull one off the shelf and the guy said, 'Don't touch it.'

"I said, 'Why not?'

"The professor said, 'They're first editions.'

"I said, 'If you can't take them off the shelf, then how do you read them?'

"And he said, 'They're not for reading.'

"That's crazy. Books you can't read. They're just paper. They mean nothing if you can't read the words, if you can't be immersed in the story like we used to be sitting with Mom out in the woods under the big pine trees.

"I guess I just didn't get it."

"Have you ever written anything yourself, stories or poems?"

"No, but I used to paint. I could always draw."

"Why'd you stop painting?"

"When I was taking medicine, I just couldn't do it. I couldn't think of anything to draw. I couldn't decide on simple colors. I used to stop taking my medicine on purpose, or take twice as much, just to see what it would do.

"I liked it though, painting. Every word you speak has been spoken before. Almost everything you do has been done before, by someone, somewhere, in the history of time. But a painting, any painting, is unique. No one, ever, has made those exact strokes of the brush, put together the exact colors the same way.

"But you have to take it for what it is. People think they can achieve some type of immortality through art, painting, writing a book, music. That's horseshit. There's no immortality through that crap. Nobody really gives a damn about it."

"You still haven't told me why you stopped painting."

"Well, I'm sure it sounds weird, but my work actually started getting some attention. An old lady, art teacher, took me under her wing. As soon as that happened, everything changed. The definition of art includes its separation from what other people think about it. If the art is created with other peoples' thoughts inside the mind of the artist at the time of creation, then it isn't art at all. It's something else. I don't know what to call it.

"I think that's what happened. It wasn't the same as it had been, and I knew it never would be again.

"People think art and mathematics are at opposite ends of the spectrum. That's wrong, unless the spectrum is a circle. It all got weird in my brain, maybe it was the blue jelly, but I couldn't look at the canvas, or touch the brush to the paint without seeing numbers in my head. Two plus two equals four. Two what? Four what? Inches? Ideas? Pills? Dollars? Catastrophic future world events foreseen years ahead by my hand blindly sliding mixed colors across pure white?

"Shit if I know. Is that a good answer?"

I slipped on my shoes and walked back to the chair. The chip in the lens of the doctor's glasses was gone. I hadn't noticed earlier, distracted by the white tissue paper with the red dot. Maybe they were different glasses. Or maybe I'd imagined the chip. That was always a possibility. My head was hot again, for no reason.

"Tell me about your employment history."

"Now there's a boring question.

"Construction, mostly. Carpenter work, roofing. It

was safe, and I could always find work because I worked hard. I learned young, and after a while it's hard to switch to something else. Besides, I like to build things. I like to see what I've done at the end of the day. Not everyone, at quittin' time, can look at what they've done that day and be proud of it. Hell, most of 'em can't see what they've done, not really.

"Four or five years ago I went through emergency medical technician training. You know, EMT, the guys that ride around in the ambulances. Now that was a crazy job. Sit around all day smoking cigarettes and drinking coffee waiting for some poor bastard to run his car into a telephone pole or choke on a chicken bone.

"I'll tell you why I finally quit. I'd seen enough dead people in car wrecks to last the rest of my life, but the last straw was when this old man fell over unconscious in his trailer. He was about four hundred pounds, covered with a bright red rash. He smelled like sour milk.

"I was down on my knees giving the guy mouth to mouth, and you know what he did? The son-of-a-bitch threw up into my mouth. I could taste it for months. That was the end for me. I'd rather work in the sun and see what my hands have built at the end of the day."

"You told me earlier about your problems sleeping. Have you always had problems sleeping?"

"I guess so, but nothing as radical as my brother and father. Sometimes they could go a week only getting out of bed to take a piss. And then they could go days and days without closing an eye. I was never that bad. I just can't ever get below the tired surface. I can't seem to really sleep deep. I think about things.

"My father used to say, 'There's two ways to live: you can sleep with one eye open all the time and never really rest, or you can sleep deeply and pray.'

"I guess I'm the first way."

"When do you remember first knowing there was something wrong with your father?"

"We just always knew. It's like asking, when was the first time you realized your mother had brown hair?

"When I was six years old, the old man woke me up one morning at four-thirty in the morning. He told me I was going deer hunting. It was time for me to kill my first deer. He had never talked about it before. It was out of the blue.

"He got me up, made me get dressed, put on my little boots, and we got in the truck. It was cold as hell. My shoulders were shaking. I could feel my teeth touching up and down.

"He was haulin' ass over dirt roads with the windows down, a shotgun between us on the seat. I'd never shot a shotgun before. I didn't want to kill a deer. I didn't want to kill anything.

"He was out of his head. Talkin' crazy shit about bein' a man, about the first taste of blood. I didn't even have a jacket.

"We finally got out to a place in the woods. We walked in the light of the early morning until we got to a deer shack, just a little camouflaged shack covered with branches, one open window hole, with a wooden bench inside.

"We sat on that hard bench. My daddy smelled like whiskey. I shook all over.

"'Stop shakin', pussy,' he said.

"I remember it. I remember the sound of the words. A whisper. A hatred.

"So we sat there, and I prayed no deer would come. I prayed to the Jesus my mother told me about. And through the little open window, out in the distance between the trees, I saw a big buck. My daddy had his head down. The buck moved slowly, cautious, raising his head and tasting the wind with his nose. I hoped my father wouldn't see it. I hoped he wouldn't look up.

"But he did. He looked up and saw the buck. We watched it get closer, and then closer."

"'Lift the gun,' my father whispered.

"I laid the barrel across the window ledge. The butt of

the gun touched my shoulder. My father pointed the barrel at the deer. I couldn't stop shaking. I couldn't make it stop.

"'Steady,' he said, 'keep it steady.'

"I could feel the tears rolling down my cold cheeks, wet in the breeze.

"And he said, 'Shoot, boy. Shoot the son-of-a-bitch.'

"'I don't want to, Daddy,' I said.

"And my father turned his eyes to me. He said, 'I don't give a fuck what you want. In this world you don't do what you want. You do what you have to.'

"I pulled the trigger. It knocked me over backward onto the dirt floor. My father screamed and busted through the door outside. I got up and stood at the window. The big buck was on the ground. He was still alive, flailing around, trying to get up. My father shot him again. He reloaded and shot him again.

"And when the deer was dead, my father punched a hole with his knife and stuck his hand inside the animal. He walked over to where I stood in the window and he rubbed the blood on my face, sticking his finger in my mouth so I could taste the red iron taste of the dead animal."

We were quiet for a while. I felt my tongue circle my lower lip remembering the taste and the smell. You didn't have to wonder whether that son-of-a-bitch was crazy.

There was no such thing as a certain day when my father's insanity became clear. It was who he was.

"Did I tell you about the time the old man got the furniture store?"

"No."

"He came up with this great idea to run a furniture store. It was going to be the answer to everything. Somehow he talked the bank into mortgaging the house to the hilt and used the money to buy this furniture store downtown. It had a big glass window storefront, tables, chairs, beds, everything.

"Dad started going to work like a normal businessman. He put on a shirt and tie and left every morning sharp at seven o'clock. He was on the upswing, taking his medication, telling funny stories. The world started to seem like a normal place.

"And then the phone rang one Wednesday afternoon. The police chief asked Mom to come to the furniture store. We loaded up in the old blue Nova and headed to town. Mom didn't drive fast. She knew whatever waited for us would still be there when we arrived.

"You should've seen it. The crazy old bastard had moved every stick of furniture out onto the sidewalk. It was all set up nice and neat, tables and matching chairs together, bedroom sets in the right places.

"The old man was inside. We stood in the doorway with the police chief. The entire store was empty. The old man had turned it into a basketball court. He'd spray-painted free throw lines and a half-court circle on the white floor. He'd nailed up a basketball goal on each end, and there he was, no shirt, barefoot, dribbling a basketball around with this crazy-ass look on his face.

"'Look,' he said. 'Think how much money we can make. We'll charge two dollars at the door. Joel can work the concession stand. The kids in town will have a place to play ball. We'll have three separate leagues, different age groups. From little bitty kids to teenagers. I don't know why I didn't think of it before.'

"After that, Dad went away for a while."

"Was your sister there that day?"

"I don't remember."

"I looked over my notes, I must have made a mistake. You said Lisa was born when you were twelve, and your dad died when you were twenty-one. Lisa would have been nine. And then you said you haven't seen her in a long time because she left. How old was she when she left? Was it before or after your dad died?"

"I don't know. It all runs together. She must've left a few years after Dad died. Maybe it was before."

"Did she come to the funeral?"

"I don't think so. I don't really remember.

"You've got a piece of toilet paper on your chin."

He reached up and rubbed his right hand across his chin until his finger touched the paper. It fell off and floated like a little parachute down to the notepad.

"Why didn't you tell me earlier?" he asked with a tone of irritation.

"I didn't notice it before."

"Excuse me a minute."

The doctor stood and walked out of the room. He was probably looking for a mirror. People are strange. Why would the doctor care so much about how he looked in front of me, an inmate being evaluated for mental problems, in a local county jail on a Thursday morning? He'd probably notice the stain on his shirt in the mirror, and the gray hair at his temples. Maybe he'd see his face, really see his own face, for the first time in years.

We stop seeing the people we know, especially ourselves. Once our split-second natural instinct of recognition occurs, we don't see anymore after that. We move to the next thing. But occasionally, maybe on a random Thursday morning in a dirty mirror, we get a glimpse of ourselves as strangers see us. We stare at lines unseen, features blurred by time.

Alone in the room I took the opportunity to stand and look down at the doctor's notes and papers on the other side of the wire mesh.

"Subject's thought pattern scattered, jumping from one topic to the next. Occasionally contradictory. Emotional swings. Obvious anger and frustration demonstrated through facial expressions, redness in face, speech pattern. There are instances of attempts at manipulation, but accounting for the subject's intelligence level, the possibility exists of more subtle forms of manipulation. However, the subject continues to appear cooperative and honest. Under his family circumstances, and the pattern of physical abuse, the subject has developed a true belief in his role as protector of younger and weaker family members."

I heard a noise and sat down. The doctor opened the door. I don't think he saw what I was doing. Dr. Andrews sat back in his chair. On his chin, where the toilet paper had been, I could see a tiny shimmer of fresh red blood. He couldn't stop the bleeding. On his shirt I could see wetness on the stain. Dr. Andrews had tried to clean it off with water. The stain was still visible, but not as dark as before.

"Do you have any tattoos or scars?"

"Do I have to answer that?"

"You don't have to answer anything, Joel. Your lawyers requested this evaluation."

"No, I don't have any tattoos. Danny used to believe when we're born, the hospital tattoos a small barcode on your ass. Too small to see. He believed every car, every government building, every airport and bus station, has a barcode reader built into the doorframes. The government tracks our movements from the day we're born, everywhere we go, and keeps the information in computers. They can draw a map of our movements from the day we're born to the day we die."

"Do you believe that?"

"It makes sense, but I don't see how the scanners could read the barcode through my pants. Hell, the lady at the grocery store sometimes has to pass the cereal box over the damn thing three or four times to get a reading. And the cereal box doesn't wear blue jeans."

"Have you ever had any homosexual experiences?"

"No."

"Have you ever thought about it?"

"Well, not really. My dad hated gays worse than blacks, or Jews, or Mexicans. He called 'em fags.

"I never could understand how you could hate people

like that. I mean, maybe some gay people are messed up, but I think most of them are just naturally attracted to their own sex. I mean, if you show me, or any other heterosexual man, photographs of a vagina, just a closeup picture of a vagina, we'll have a physical reaction. We'll get an erection. We don't even have to see the face that goes along with the vagina. It just happens.

"What if you were growing up, and your friends were sneaking dirty magazines, and you just didn't have that physical reaction to the pictures of the women? What if you had a physical reaction to a dick, a photograph of a dick? It just happened. You couldn't help that anymore than I could help being attracted to a woman's genitals. God knows they're not pretty. There's just a reason for it. I don't have to understand the reason, but I also don't have to hate people whose minds and bodies react differently than mine. It's as stupid as hating someone because of the color of their hair.

"And I never could figure out how religious people could hate like that. I mean, if you believe in God, and you believe God is all knowing, and all caring, and all powerful. And God has a plan for all his children. How could you hate someone because God gave them a different color skin, or made them fall in love with a person of a different race, or made them have a physical reaction to a photograph of a dick, or even made them born in a different country in a different religion? Maybe a religion that worships a different God.

"I don't understand. Hell, seventeen percent of sheep prefer to have sexual contact with their own sex. What's that all about?"

"Have you ever been in love?"

"There's no such thing as love. There's dependence. There's survival. There's fear of being alone. There's lust. But there's no such thing as love. We made it up. Just like we made up God. The idea of love lets us feel better, like there's a force outside ourselves we can't control. It's not our fault. We can blame it on love."

"That's a cynical view, don't you think?"

"Yes, I do. I almost got married once. Her name was Ann. Did you ever pass by something on the road you just couldn't stop looking at? Couldn't stop thinking about? That's what she was, literally. I passed her one day. She was sittin' on the hood of a car, short pants, one of those sleeveless T-shirts. Yellow.

"I turned around and went back. You might not have thought she was pretty, but I couldn't pass her by.

"It didn't work out."

"What happened?"

"Lots of things happened. My own happiness became

completely dependent upon her happiness. Completely. And when she figured out the power, she couldn't help but abuse it. It took more and more to make her happy. More than I could do."

"How did she get along with your family?"

"She didn't. At first it was O.K., but eventually she pushed herself between me and my mother. There was friction. Always choose against the person who makes you choose. People who love you don't force you to make choices like that."

"I thought you said there was no such thing as love."

"I did. You know what I mean."

"So who broke up with who?"

"I just told her it wasn't a possibility. None of it. How could I have children? It would be the ultimate selfish act, passing along my blood to a little baby. Besides that, I couldn't allow the control that comes with the commitment.

"In the end, I hated her. We had an argument while we were out of town. We broke up and then had to drive home together in the car for three hours. There was nothing left to talk about. We just rode in silence for three hours. I couldn't stand sitting next to her. It was hard to imagine why I hadn't been able to pass her by that day. In the end, there was nothing good about it, but it probably wasn't her fault."

"Whose fault was it?"

"Who knows? I still think about her. I remember seeing a family picture in her mom's house. It was a photograph of the four generations of women, great-grandmother, grandmother, mother, and Ann when she was about seventeen. I remember looking at the picture a long time and wondering if those other women had ever looked like Ann, creamy skin, long hair, the tightness of being young.

"Did you ever read *The Last Gentleman* by Walker Percy? There's a line in that book: 'Lucky is the man who does not secretly believe every possibility is open to him.'

"It looks like any other sentence, hidden away in the flow of a paragraph, surrounded on a page in the middle of a chapter. But it isn't. It isn't just another sentence. It can change the way you live. Remember when I told you I will never dunk a basketball? It's an opportunity unavailable to me. It always will be. If I fail to recognize that fact, a simple fact of nature, I could piss away great quantities of time and effort. Time and effort better utilized in accomplishing something possible.

"It's not as easy as it sounds. There are many things in this life, difficult to attain, well worth fighting for. The trick lies in the recognition. I was forced to recognize the fact that Ann, being married to her, holding our babies, would never be a possibility. I could have married her, worked hard, built a house, conceived a child, spent great quantities of time and effort, only to discover the inevitable. It was not an opportunity open to me, and it never could have been.

"You have to look closely at the quote from the book. He says 'Lucky is the man.' 'Lucky' is a strange word to use. There doesn't seem to be anything lucky about a man working hard to understand himself. But maybe he means lucky by birth. Some men are born to understand the concept eventually, and others are destined to spend their lives wallowing around lost in the idea.

"He also says 'secretly believe.' It's not just what we admit we believe that's important. Those things inside us, those things we secretly believe, they run the show. Those are the beliefs that seep out through the surface and reveal themselves in everything we do. We can't just disown the idea as irrational or irrelevant. We have to actually disbelieve to the core.

"In the last part he says 'open to him.' 'Every possibility is open to him.' Not just the opportunities that appear realistically possible to us, or the opportunities that seem fruitful, but all those endless possibilities each of us dreams are open before us, every single day, every turn. Like Danny."

I felt a tightness in my chest. Tight enough to put my hand against it. I couldn't catch my breath. It came in short pulls. It was like my lungs were suddenly the size of a fist, balled up and squeezed inward. My eyes closed with the dizziness. It wasn't the first time it happened.

"What's the matter?" I heard a voice say. "What's the matter?" again.

I just concentrated on the next breath, a little bigger than the one before. Forcing the fist open one half-inch at a time. In, and then out again. Back in, a little deeper than before. Loosen the fist, open the spaces between the fingers. Feel the dizziness reach the bottom of the hole, and then slowly climb upwards, until I know where I am, know what to say.

"I'm O.K."

"What happened?"

"I'm O.K. I just couldn't catch my breath. It's back now."

"Do you need some water?"

"No. I don't need anything."

We sat quiet for a few minutes. I could feel the doctor's eyes all over me. I could almost hear his mind working.

"I had this dream the other night. Me and Ann were at a Little League baseball game. We were sitting in the bleachers, people all around us. I looked over at her, and she was bare-chested. I turned away, took my eyes away from her as long as I could. When I couldn't stand it anymore, I looked back at her. I looked down at her breasts. They were covered with flies. Her tits were covered with black flies. And she just sat there and watched the game.

"What the hell does that mean?"

"I don't know."

"How am I doing so far?"

"What do you mean?"

"I mean, in the evaluation, how am I doing so far? I know I'm a bit scattered, even occasionally contradictory or emotional, but isn't that the definition of a human being?"

I used the doctor's words. I used the same words he wrote in his notes. He studied me, wondering if it was just a coincidence, or if I'd seen what he'd written? Or maybe he even considered the possibility I was one step ahead of him: inside his mind more than he was inside mine.

"What's that smell?" I asked.

"What smell?"

"Doesn't it smell like something's burning?"

"I don't smell anything."

The doctor tilted his head upwards and sniffed. For an instant he reminded me of that big buck in the woods with his nose in the air. Why would my senses tell me something was burning if nothing was burning at all?

"Danny was always messin' with fire," I said.

"I think it's time we talked about Danny."

"When he was a kid, just a little kid, he would come up to us with his fist closed tight and say, 'I got fire in my hand.'

"He was fascinated by it. He always had matches or lighters. I think that's why he started smokin', so he could have a reason to be around it. So he could touch it and run his finger through the flame.

"He was always smokin' cigarettes, just like the old man. Chain smokin'. He even held the cigarette the same way as the old man, kinda cupped it like it was a secret."

"Tell me more about Danny's relationship with your father."

"It was complicated. Danny only saw the good things. He only saw the possibilities. Possibilities that didn't really exist, but they existed for Danny.

"They looked alike. I think they saw themselves in each other.

"Explaining crazy people is impossible. You can't separate the real from the unreal. Danny saw things. You couldn't tell him they didn't exist, and after a while, I couldn't be sure about anything. Maybe it was me who was delusional.

"I would try to tell him right from wrong, and then the line would move. I'd try to make him understand about our father, but it's hard to explain something you don't understand yourself.

"Danny would say crazy shit. He was scared of leaving his DNA anywhere. He was afraid of leaving a stray pubic hair somewhere, or lettin' a lonely drop of his piss fall outside the toilet. He believed people followed him around trying to get his DNA for some national database. It didn't matter how many times you told him it wasn't true. It was true for him, so it didn't matter.

"You know, how do we really know anyway? How do we know that when I see red, it's the same red you see? Why is it we believe there's only one reality, and not a different world through different eyes? It's comforting to believe there's one truth, but who the hell can really say what's rational to me was rational to Danny?"

"Was Danny able to live on his own, hold a job?"

"For short periods of time, yeah. But it wouldn't last. He was a bird with one wing, but he was crippled in a way most people couldn't see. It would have been easier, I think, if he was paralyzed, or had no legs, or something obvious. But when you're crippled with mental illness, people think it's a weakness. They think you're lazy, or dumb, or just trying to get something for nothing. It's hard to understand.

"Danny believed there was a code word to get out of speeding tickets. He believed the code word changed every month and the rich people would be notified of the new word through the newspaper. He would read the paper everyday trying to find the hidden code word. And then, when he thought he'd figured it out, he'd intentionally speed around town until he was pulled over. When the cop would come up to the window Danny would say something stupid like 'hamburger' or 'green apple.' He'd say it over and over, trying to fit the word into normal conversation. 'I'm on my way to get a hamburger, officer,' or 'It sure is a nice day for a green apple, don't you think?'

"If it wasn't your brother, and it wasn't so crazy, you might think it was funny. But when you've got to pick him up at the police station five days in a row, it ain't funny anymore. The cops just got to the point where they'd take him in every time. He didn't even have a license. They'd hold him a while and call us to get him."

"Was he ever violent?"

"Most of the time, no. The drugs would get him all screwed up. He was on and off his medication, and in between he self-medicated with whatever he could get his hands on: crack, whiskey, marijuana.

"He always talked about the seasons inside him. The drugs would throw the seasons off. He would be way up with grand ideas and plans. Then he would spiral down to winter. Sometimes to the point of a fetus, rolled up in a ball somewhere, unable to even decide to eat or get up to take a shit. It was just a constant cycle, and toward the end, the seasons would come and go so fast it was hard to tell the difference anymore.

"And by the way, I hope you don't think I expect you to bless what I did. You can't bless what you can't understand. It's like I said earlier, don't be so sure your reality is the real one. Any conclusion you reach is based upon some idea of a baseline. If that baseline isn't what you think it is, or doesn't exist at all, then there's nothing conclusive about your conclusions, good or bad. It's just as irrational as believing people in white coats are in the bathroom down the hall using tweezers to pick up that hair you dropped earlier when you were looking in the mirror for the little cut on your chin."

The burnt smell was gone. The doctor was taking furious notes, careful to tilt the pad enough for me not to get a good look. His face had changed just a bit, it's hard to explain, but something about the look made me stare. I wanted to draw it. The lines were clear.

"Can I have a piece of paper?"

Without asking me why, the doctor tore off a sheet of paper from the pad. There was a one-inch space between the bottom of the wire screen and the metal table top. Dr. Andrews slid the yellow sheet through the space to my side of the room. I already had a fine-tip black ink pen.

The first line is the most important. Don't start until you see where you're going. Don't begin until the image is set in your mind. You can't draw what you can't see inside. A drawing is more than the mirror image of a photograph. That's the reason men have museums full of paintings, even after the invention of the camera. Photographs will never take the place of paintings or drawings. There's something magic about the mind in between the subject and the creation.

I drew the first line.

"Tell me about the day Danny died."

"It was like any other day. It was a Saturday. Danny loved to go fishin'. He loved it."

The doctor looked across at me. He saw the black line on the white page, but he didn't say anything, or change the look on his face.

"He wanted to go fishin' that day. We went down to a pond off Highway 4. We'd been there before. Catfish, a few bass. Pine trees all around.

"It was just me and Danny. Mom was out of town at her sister's house in Crandon. She wasn't supposed to be back until Monday."

The lines on the page flowed from my hand. It was the first time in a long time, but the picture was set in my head. It was like tracing. I looked down, and then up again, as I answered the doctor's question.

"We just had two cane poles and some worms. Danny never gave a damn about catching anything. He just loved to sit there. He loved to talk and watch the red cork bob on top of the dirty brown water.

"It was a gray December day, cool, but not cold. Danny had short sleeves. We sat together on the bank of the pond. I could see the scratches up his arms. He would cut himself. When he was bad off, he'd scratch up his arms with 'most anything, broken glass, leaving crisscross scratches up and down his arms from the elbow to the wrist.

"They call it self-mutilation, but I'm sure you know that."

The background of the doctor's face melted into the face itself. It's hard to explain. The longer I stared, the more details I could see, the more connection between one piece and the other, until there were no pieces. The eyes spread out for me, through the cheeks, to the edges of the mouth, and then like a stream flowed back to the vertical of the bridge of the nose and circled over again.

Usually, I would've been afraid the subject would move, if only barely, and break the moment, end the dependence. But I didn't feel any fear.

"It was late afternoon. Danny started crying. There was no reason I could see. He was sittin' down the bank, maybe twenty or thirty yards away at the time, and he started crying.

"I couldn't stop lookin' at him. I just couldn't turn away anymore. It was his favorite thing to do, fishin'. But he couldn't keep himself from crying, scars up and down his arms. He just wasn't for this world, and I knew the time had come.

"I didn't plan it when I woke up that mornin'. I didn't have a day marked on the calendar. There's a time for everything, and it was time for Danny. There was no point anymore. He wasn't going to get better, and the world wasn't going to change. And he knew it."

My words seemed to float over the doctor like a cool white sheet, settling down on him softly. The color of the room was odd and pale as the picture of the man across from me took form on the paper under my hand. It was an old, welcome feeling.

"And so you know what Danny says, sittin' there on the bank of the pond, twenty or thirty yards away? You know what he says?

"He says, 'Joel, today's the day.'

"That's what he said.

"We were quiet for a few minutes, looking at our red corks on the top of the pond. Just two brothers on a Saturday, fishin' together. And I said, 'I know, Danny. I know.'

"We stayed there a while longer, until it was dark, and then drove home. We didn't speak, but there was nothing uneasy. In fact, it was the very opposite. We had said all that needed to be said. The hard part was over, the knowing, the recognizing, it was done.

"We got back to the house and put away the fishing poles. Danny sat down on the couch and started to cry again. He held the pistol in his lap. He was crying for the seconds, the minutes, he had to wait in this world. But he couldn't do it. He just couldn't do it for himself.

"I remember it was cold in the room. It was winter, and Danny had shit his pants again. The living room was dark, but the kitchen light was on, a yellowish light."

My hand on the page had a mind of its own. I was drawing without looking down. I couldn't take my eyes from the doctor's face. It was the clearest thing I had ever seen, like my eyes had never worked right before. Like I was seeing things I should have seen all along.

One line, and then the next, and then the shoulders, and the scar, and the chest, back up to the eyes, and the bone structure underneath the skin.

"So I went and got my gun. I stood in the doorway to the kitchen. And I looked at my little brother. And I thought to myself, 'The strong are always the chosen. They choose themselves. They don't wait.'

"And I counted my steps: one, two, three, four, five, into the living room. Six, seven.

"And Danny looked up at me. He looked up at me and smiled. And I pointed the gun at my brother's head. For a moment I wanted to touch his hair. Just touch it. And then I pulled the trigger."

The picture was finished. I looked down and saw what I had done.

"Could you do that Dr. Andrews? Could you smile with a gun to your head? It was all the proof I needed. It was like the day I tried to let the monkey out of the cage. It may have been against the law, but it wasn't wrong. It wasn't wrong when I did it, and isn't wrong now."

I pushed the picture through the slit between the wire mesh and the metal table. I turned it right side up so the doctor could see himself. He didn't touch the paper with his hands, but his eyes stayed on his eyes, maybe seeing himself in a way the mirror can't show.

"I put the gun down on the table and called the police. I walked outside and sat down on the cement steps of the porch. It was cooler than earlier. My brother was inside dead.

"It was so loud. Louder than I thought it would be. That was the part I didn't expect. My ears were ringing on the porch like a hum over everything, and there was blood on my hand, but I didn't wipe it off. I just left it there.

"I remember seeing a penny. It was dark, but in the light from the kitchen and the streetlight I could see a shiny penny on the sidewalk at the bottom of the steps.

"My father believed if you find a penny, and it's heads-up, you've got good luck. You know what? No matter how many times you tell yourself something like that is crazy, there's always a part of you that wants to believe.

"My father also believed if you find a penny heads-down it brings you bad luck. He got to where he was so afraid of finding a penny heads-down, and he believed it so much, he wouldn't look down at all."

The doctor wasn't watching me. He was still looking at the picture. He finally looked back up and asked, "Did you look at the penny?"

"Yeah, I did. It was heads-up. I put it in my pocket right about the time the first police car showed up. They threw me to the ground and stuck a knee in my back, but I knew the penny was still there, down at the bottom of my blue jeans pocket. It's probably still there now, in the storage room down the hall with the rest of my clothes."

"Did you give a statement to the police?"

"No, I didn't see the point."

We stared at each other for at least thirty seconds. I think he was trying to figure out something. Finally he lifted his arm and looked at the black digital watch on his wrist.

"We're out of time today, Joel. I'll come back on Monday morning, around nine o'clock."

I watched him put the reports and pages of notes in the binder. He covered my drawing by placing a notebook on top. Then he picked them up together carefully and placed both inside the binder with everything else.

I actually looked forward to seeing the doctor again. We need things to look forward to, no matter what they are: sex, food, a football game, whatever the hell gets you to the next moment and beyond. It's easy to run out of things to look forward to in jail.

I stepped through the door into the usual meeting room and was surprised to see my mother sitting on the other side of the screen next to Dr. Andrews. She looked so small and tired. She put her hand to the screen, and I touched my hand to hers, the cold metal in between.

"*Hey, Baby,*" she whispered.

"Are you O.K., Momma? I didn't know you were coming."

"I arranged for her to come, Joel," the doctor said. His voice was hard, and I knew there was a reason.

Momma leaned back in her chair. She appeared to

fold into herself. When you're a kid, everything seems big. Maybe she was always tiny. It made me wonder what the pine tree place would look like to me now, through grown-up eyes. I'd rather remember it the way it looked before. The way it seemed through little-boy eyes, big and wonderful. How long do pine trees live anyway?

The doctor's brown binder was open in front of him. He wore a short-sleeved shirt again. The dark black hair on his arms stood out even more than before. I noticed he wasn't wearing his wedding ring, and I looked to his eyes for a reason, but they were hard like his voice.

"Joel, I met with your mother like I told you I would. It's standard to gather background information and family history. I know this is a difficult time for all of you. Your family has been through a lot, but I have a job to do, and the court expects me to do it to the best of my ability."

As the doctor spoke, my mother looked down at her hands folded in her lap. I watched her face, listening to the doctor's words, trying my best to figure out what it was all about.

"Your mother has something to tell you, Joel, and she asked me to be here to talk about it."

"Are you sick, Mom?" It was the first thing that came to my mind.

"No, no, nothing like that. She's not sick."

"Well, just tell me."

We waited, and then my mother looked up from her hands and said simply, "*Your father is not your real father.*"

I heard the words. I could feel the doctor's eyes on me like they'd been before, searching for something to write down on his pad. I didn't move.

"What are you talking about?" I asked, my voice steady on a straight line, no ups and downs of inflection, nothing for the doctor to write about.

"*Your father, the man you grew up calling your father, isn't your natural father.*

"*I should have told you before, I know, but the time was never right. It was never the right time.*"

I just watched her mouth move. She was small and tired, shrunken, but my mother's eyes were still bright and strong, except now she was crying. Not loud and pitiful, not for show, but just crying, the little tears leaving her eyes down to the cheeks, and her fingers reaching up and spreading them away into a soft shimmer of wetness. She had practiced the words, but I could tell the practice was a waste of time. Now she was just telling me the story.

"*I got pregnant with you when I was sixteen. The man had a wife and a family. He was a good man. I didn't want to ruin him. Your daddy thought you were his. He loved you in his way, the only way he knew how to love. He put a roof*

over our heads. He asked me to marry him, and I did. I was
sixteen, Joel, and I had a baby coming, no job, no education.
I don't know if you'll understand."

I can't describe exactly how I felt. It was much like
being dead. There are a few conversations in a lifetime
worth remembering. I just listened and hoped it would
end soon, hoped I would know what to think. As the
words came from my mother's mouth I tried to line them
up like organizing clothes in a chest-of-drawers. The
socks in one drawer, shirts in another, neatly folded,
tucked away.

"He never knew you weren't his, but he might have sus-
pected. I don't know. I never told him. Daniel was his baby,
of course."

The tears silently rolled down her face like raindrops,
but she kept her eyes on mine and her words clear. There
were so many questions, so many answers, and they
would lead to new questions and more new questions
until there would be no more answers.

"Your real father was John Clayton, the preacher. Do
you remember him? He lived down the street from us when
you were a little boy. He moved there so he could be near
you. So he could look after you. He had two little girls. One
was in your grade at school."

To myself, out loud, I said, "I was in his house once."

"I know. When you got hurt falling out of the tree. I'm

glad you remember. He died when you were nine years old.
Something was wrong with his heart. I couldn't believe it
when they told me. He was only thirty. I never imagined
him dying.

"Don't think bad of him, Joel. He never thought of you
as a mistake. He loved you. I wish things would have been
different, but they weren't. They are what they are."

Up until her last sentence I held an unnatural control.
The swings inside me were fast. I thought about the day in
the preacher's house, the feeling. I thought about whether
I could see my face in his face, and how he could leave me
in the house with that crazy man, and how my mother felt
standing in the doorway at the church watching my real
father give a Sunday sermon to his only son. I wished I
could remember what he said because it must have been
worth remembering, a message passed between father to
son, and I missed it. I missed it all.

It was my mother's last sentence that ended my control. "They are what they are." And they can never be
changed. And we can never go back again. And I can never
know John Clayton. And who was the man I called father?
And who was my mother screwing at sixteen? And who
exactly am I?

My teeth clinched together and I said, "Who did I kill,
Mom? Who did I kill? Can you tell me that. I thought I
knew what was happening to Danny. I thought I under-

stood it because it was happening to me, too. But I didn't know at all. I had no right to be the one."

I stood up from my chair and leaned my face near the screen looking down at my mother. I'd never talked to her like that before, but I couldn't stop it.

"Who exactly am I? I've dedicated my life to not being the man I called father, and I was never him all along. I killed my brother to save him from something I don't even understand, that I can't understand. If I hadn't killed Danny, would you have told me? If I wasn't sitting in jail with Danny's blood on my hands, would you have ever told me?"

My voice rose up with each question. I don't remember breathing.

"Please sit down, Joel."

The words startled me. The sight of him when I turned my head shocked the shit out of me. Where had he come from?

I sat down, and we were all very quiet for a time. Questions would pass my mind but not come out in words. Finally I asked, "How could you have that crazy man's babies? How could you, knowing the poison in his blood? How could you do that to Danny and Lisa? I've hated my sister, and admired her, for leaving us. And now I can't confess to understand why she did what she did."

My mother squinted up her face and looked at me like I'd hurt her on purpose. Like I was the one telling her crazy shit I should've told her before it was too late. She fought against the contortions of her face, against completely losing control of her sadness. I'd never seen her that way.

The doctor said, "Your mother told me about Lisa. I know the truth, Joel."

The truth is a strange thing. It doesn't change. Only we change. "Lucky is the man who doesn't secretly believe every possibility is open to him." There must be a foundation of acknowledgment at a basic fundamental level. A penny is a penny. It is what it is, and only what it is. If a man cannot, or will not, grasp the understanding, nothing else is sure.

"Lisa was the name your mother gave to the baby girl stillborn when you were twelve years old."

My mother put her face in her hands. Her body shook, but there was no way to reach her. No way to hold her on the other side of the metal screen to stop the shaking. Why would she tell the doctor that? Maybe it was easier to believe than the truth. My eyes closed, and I searched for the image of my little sister, early in the morning, sitting up in her bed, pretending to read her book out loud. Blonde hair hanging down on the sides of her face. The little hands clenched on the edges of the book. And the voice. The sweetness of the made-up words of a child on a new morning.

I felt the tears come to my own eyes. Why had the man I called father never loved me? Why had my real father left me alone? The most powerful human instinct, more powerful than the desire to survive, is the instinct of protecting our children. Animals will die without hesitation to protect their young. They will sacrifice their very lives for their babies. How could my fathers, both of them, different and the same, feel nothing for me, drop me off at the end of a dirt road and drive away?

There was a scream from down the hall in the holding cell. It was loud and piercing. The scream of a man in a nightmare, and I looked up to see the doctor and my mother looking at me for some explanation. I cannot explain the scream or where it came from. I cannot explain anything.

"Why would you let him take me hunting? I was just a little kid."

"*The day you were born was the best day of my life, Joel. When I held you wrapped up in the white blanket, with that little blue hat on your head, it was like nothing else mattered. It was like everything before was right, and I'd always be able to go back to that moment.*

"*And when Danny was born, I had my boys. You were*

like a little man, Joel. A little man there for me and Danny. I knew it wasn't right, but you were all I had. And when Danny started having problems, and then John died, and then Daddy got worse, it was just you.

"*I could see what it did to you, but I couldn't stop it. It's not your fault. Does any of that make sense? I'm sorry.*"

The doctor's voice seemed to come from the sky. "Joel, when people, particularly children, are placed in traumatic circumstances, the mind will take drastic steps to cope. Oftentimes the result is the creation of delusions, a fantasy world, imaginary friends, a separate reality. You told me Lisa was hope. At twelve years old, under the pressure of your father and your brother's mental illness, in your role as protector of your mother and Danny, you weren't equipped to deal with the death of your sister. The death of your hope. So you've allowed her to live inside your mind."

"I know why you're doing this, Mother. You can't change anything."

"I asked your mother about the time you said you were arrested for public intoxication in the train car. It wasn't you, Joel. It was Danny who was arrested for public intoxication in the train car. I checked it out with criminal records."

Something was going on. It was hard to tell what. Was

I supposed to play along? Had there been some backroom deal struck while the judge and the lawyers played poker at the hunting camp? Was I supposed to fake crazy? I almost expected the doctor to wink at me. But after all, there were no blue jelly balls in my veins, floating. I didn't have the poison blood of the crazy son-of-a-bitch who died in my mother's bed.

So whose blood did I have, and did it matter, if the deal was done? I took a moment to look slowly around the room for the reflection of the lens of a little video camera. Where would it be? Maybe in the blue ink pen, or the silver screw in the doctor's glasses. No, too shaky. Maybe in the ceiling, or the light fixture. Maybe nowhere at all.

"What are you looking for, Joel?"

"Deal or no deal, I can't pretend my sister didn't exist. I can't blame Danny for the things I've done. I killed my brother. I knew what I was doing, and I'd do it again. Don't you want to know what I did, Mom? Don't you want to know how I killed him? He was your son, too, you know. Maybe he wasn't your firstborn, and maybe he wasn't the child of a preacher-man who messed around with a sixteen-year-old girl while his wife sat home with his baby, and maybe he was the son of the most fucked-up man God ever made, but he was still your son.

"Speaking of God, what kind of God does this to

people? Explain it to me. What kind of sick God kills babies, and makes Danny mutilate himself up and down his arms with a busted beer bottle, and lets me lay on the couch of my real father's home ten minutes so I can know the rest of my life what I couldn't have? What kind of shit is that? Don't you want to know how your big, brave, first-born pointed a gun at your second son's head? Well, I'm gonna tell you, and you're gonna listen.

"He was crying, Mom. The snot was runnin' down his nose..."

And I stopped in the middle of the sentence. I just stopped and looked at her. I came from her. I came out of her, into the world, on a certain day, for a certain reason. And the nurse cleaned me up, washed my mother's juices from my skin, wrapped me in a blanket, and put a little blue hat on my head, and my mother held me, and for once, maybe the only time in her life, it made sense. And now, twenty-nine years later, she's buried everyone she loved except me. And we sit in jail, a cold metal screen between our hands.

"Danny told me he loved you. It was the last thing he said, Mom. He loved you, and he'll see you in heaven. That's what he said."

I looked at the doctor. His left hand jotted notes. I didn't bother to sneak a look. I felt sorry for him. Dr. Ellis Andrews wasn't the kind of man to take off his wedding ring. There were dark circles under his eyes. He hadn't slept much. It must be hard to put other people's problems ahead of your own.

"Sometimes, at night, when I'm sleepin' in my cell, I can hear this dog barking outside. I know it's not possible, but I always think it's my dog, the one with dad when he wrecked the truck down the street. Do you remember that dog?"

"*I do.*"

"Why didn't he have a name?"

"*I guess he didn't need one.*"

"He just disappeared. He just ran away from the truck before we could get there. And he never came back. Where would he go?"

"*I don't know. He might have gotten disoriented and couldn't find his way home. Maybe somebody took him in and gave him a good place to live. He was a gentle dog. He just showed up at our house one day and we kept him.*"

"Maybe he ran away from his real home to come stay with us. Maybe he left another house in the middle of the night and found something better. Or maybe he went back. That night, when Dad wrecked the truck, maybe the dog went back to his real home. And maybe that home is right down the block from here, and that's my dog I hear barking at night."

"*I don't think so, honey. That was twenty-five years ago.*"

I don't think he'd still be alive."

"No, I guess not. Do you know where my sisters are? Mr. Clayton's younger daughter, the one in my class, I think her name was Melissa. I don't remember the older one's name. You think they have any idea they have a brother?"

"I don't know."

"It seems weird doesn't it? Their father was my father. I was in their house once. I fell out of the tree and Mr. Clayton carried me in his house and laid me down on his couch. It smelled good in there. It should've been us in that house."

"Will they let you paint here?"

"I'm just curious, Mom. Why did you hate Ann?"

"I didn't hate her."

"Yes, you did. You hated her the first day I brought her home to meet you. I thought it was because you didn't want me to ever have babies. You didn't want me to do the same thing you did to Danny and Lisa, make crazy babies, pass along the genes. But you knew I didn't have the genes. You knew all along I could have felt what you felt that day you held me at the hospital."

"She wasn't good enough for you, Joel."

"That's not it. You didn't want me to leave you alone with them. You couldn't leave, and so neither could I. How could you let me believe that all my life? How could you take me to mental doctors and make me take medications like Danny?"

"Joel, mental illness isn't always passed in bloodlines. People with no mental illness in the family can be schizophrenic, or bi-polar, or suffer from a variety of other mental conditions. Circumstances can also cause certain problems. We all react differently."

"*Can you help us?*"

"What do you mean?"

"*Can you tell the judge Joel was temporarily insane, or mentally ill, or whatever? What good will it do to have him spend the rest of his life in prison? It's just the two of us left. You can't believe he'd ever hurt anybody else. Why can't he have a life? I'll take care of him.*"

"It's not that simple, Ms. Stabler."

"*Yes, it is. Please help us. Joel's not just another case on the docket, another file at the courthouse. You can help us. What if it was your son? What if we said Danny killed himself? He would have killed himself sooner or later anyway.*"

The doctor studied my mother as she spoke. I could see his mind running in loose circles. He laid the blue ink pen on the pad of paper and rubbed his face with his left hand. There was a band of slightly whiter skin underneath the place his wedding ring used to be. Finally he said, "I think we're done for the day."

The doctor gathered up his papers. My mother stood from her chair. Her dress looked old. I'd seen her wear it a hundred times, maybe more. After all she'd told me, all she'd said, you'd think I'd see her differently, but I didn't.

"*Do you need anything?*"

"No."

"*Will they let you smoke in here? I'll bring your ciga-rettes.*"

"No thanks," I said. "No smoking and no painting in jail."

The doctor stood at the door. He put his hand in his pocket and pulled out car keys. A coin fell to the gray cement floor. I stood to see. It was a penny, a new copper penny. Everything had changed. The doctor didn't look down. He just turned and left.

SESSION IV
(Thursday, January 27th)

I slept a lot the days after my mother came to visit. Have you ever fallen down, physically? Maybe slipped on a wet spot on the floor, or tripped over something you didn't see, and fell to the ground so fast there was no time to try to break the fall? That's how it felt when my mother told me the things she told me. There was no time to break the fall.

At first, I didn't want to think about it. When I was alone, my mind would play games with me. Was it a dream, just like the dream of Ann sitting in the bleachers of the Little League field with flies covering her breasts?

After a few days, I started looking forward to seeing the doctor again. Sometimes it's hard to tell if the craziness is inside of me or on the outside, the craziness of the world. A world with no rules except the artificial, man-made rules we create. They're so fragile and brittle. One push, one hard push, and the first rule falls. After that, after the knowledge of the fall, there's not much to hold it together. What's next? Maybe Dr. Andrews isn't a doctor at all. Maybe he's my father, or my brother, or my mother's new lover, and I never really killed Danny, and this is all just a bad episode where I should have taken my medicine. But then my mind would come back to the day my father carried me into his home, and laid me on his couch, and touched my hair with his hand, and I knew it was true. His eyes were like mine. I had come from him, but that's all.

And then I couldn't catch my breath again. And my chest pounded with the hotness that rose to my head. It's hard to forget about the blue jelly balls. They'd been with me for so long. They don't just go away because they're supposed to. They don't just disappear when you learn they were never there at all.

I waited in the room for the doctor. I slowed down and thought about nothing until the air came easier, and the hotness melted away, and I couldn't feel my insides anymore. Dr. Andrews entered the room.

"Hello, Joel."

"Good morning."

He sat down to get organized. The doctor wore a white, button-down, long-sleeved shirt. More formal than before. Maybe it was his attempt to draw the line between us, doctor and patient, free man and inmate. He looked tired again, not clean shaven, with those dark circles under his eyes. The wedding ring was still missing.

"I guess you've had a lot to think about these last few days."

"I was hoping you'd tell me it was just a dream."

I watched him shuffle the papers around.

"Is time the same for everybody?" I asked.

"What do you mean?"

"Something weird happened last night. It felt like time was speeding up and slowing down, just jerkin' back and forth. So I laid down on the bed and positioned myself to see the clock. I closed my eyes and counted to sixty. When I opened my eyes, three minutes had gone by. I figured maybe I just counted slow. So I did it again. The next time, after the same count to sixty, only thirty seconds passed.

"I started thinkin', maybe time slows down and speeds up. We'd never know, would we? I mean, it's not like we can check it all the time.

"Do you believe Lisa exists?"

"Joel, the human mind is a powerful thing. You believed, without a doubt, one hundred percent, you were destined to suffer from the same mental illness you saw your entire life in your father and your brother. You believed it was your destiny, unequivocally.

"Have you ever heard of the placebo effect?"

I didn't answer.

"If you take two groups of sick people, Group A and Group B, and you give Group A medicine proven to help them, and you give Group B a sugar pill, a placebo, the results are astounding. As long as both groups are told they are receiving the real medicine, and they are convinced the real medicine will make them better, for the short-term at least, both groups improve equally. Our minds are so powerful we can actually make our bodies respond in a positive way despite the fact we are only taking worthless sugar pills.

"The opposite can also be true. If you believe, without a doubt, you are destined to be sick, your mind can make you just as sick as if you had an illness, such as a mental illness. It can be just as powerful as psychosis. It's a reverse placebo effect. In a sense, you made yourself delusional."

I thought about what he said. "Where does it stop? I mean, how can I tell now what was real, and what was a delusion?"

"You have to do that for yourself, Joel."

"Do you think Lisa is real?"

"I think Lisa was the name of the baby that died when you were twelve years old. I don't know what happened, but in your situation, you weren't able to accept her death, so your mind created a delusion. A delusion of a little sister. She was safe from your father, because she didn't exist. She was safe from the insanity. But she was there for you, to help you cope with an impossible situation. Twelve-year-old boys should be worrying about baseball games, and girls, and math tests, not protecting your mother and brother. Not being physically beaten by your father. Not wondering every night if the next morning you'll wake up with the insanity you saw in the eyes of your father and brother."

"It doesn't seem possible I drove around out west for months looking for a little sister who didn't exist. It just doesn't seem possible. I can see her in my mind, but what's weird, I can't remember what she looked like after about five years old. I can't form her face in my mind."

"That's because your mind wouldn't let her grow up. If she grew up, she might start showing the same signs Danny showed. She might become a victim of your father, the man you believed was your father."

I wanted to ask the doctor about his wedding ring, but it didn't seem like the right time.

I saw gray in his eyebrows. There was an intensity. Dr. Ellis Andrews was completely consumed by my situation. His words seemed off the cuff, but really they were researched explanations of some curious condition. Maybe I had become his diversion from whatever unhappiness he faced outside. Maybe it wasn't a sacrifice to dedicate himself to my predicament, but instead it was a relief from thinking and overthinking his private situation. It was a chance to get her face out of his mind, her words out of his ears, and his world off his shoulders.

"Joel?"

"Yes."

"Before Danny died, did he really say he loved your mother?"

"No."

"Why did you tell her that?"

"She needed it. She needed to have something good to think about."

"What do you need?"

"I need to leave this place."

"If you got out of jail, what would you do? Where would you live?"

"I'd go fishin', maybe. Or go to a place like Montana, wide open spaces. Plenty of room to think. I'd paint some of those big rolling hills. Sit out in the sunshine and just paint the hell out of it, all day long.

"I'd take some time to figure out what questions I really need answered. I wouldn't mind going to my real father's grave and just sittin' there for a while. I don't expect much from it, but I'd do it anyway. I'd like to see his name on the stone.

"Maybe go out to the pine tree place I told you about. You should go there. It's out off Highway 49. Take a left at the light, going south. Pull over next to the big cotton field. You can see the tops of the trees from the road. Walk down the side of the cotton field and there's a trail. You can't miss it. You should go."

"I don't get down that way much."

"You should. Take your kids with you."

It was slight, just a slight difference, but I could see his eyes change when I mentioned his children.

"She took 'em, didn't she?"

His left hand reached up and rubbed his forehead. **"We're here to talk about you, Joel."**

"I noticed you're not wearing your wedding ring."

The doctor turned his hand palm-down and stared at the pale skin where the ring used to be. He looked too long, unable to break away, lost for a moment. How many days in a row did he think he could go without something bad happening? Wrapping himself in a routine, waking up the same time every morning, going to work, the same cup of coffee, three-fourths full, cream, sugar, work, go home, watch the news, asleep by 10:30.

I broke the silence. "You must be a good father."

I smiled, "I know what you're thinkin'. 'How would I know?' Well you don't have to have a good father, or even be a good father, to know what one looks like. I know all I need to know."

For a moment, I thought the doctor might leave. I'd pushed him too deep, and he didn't seem able to climb out, so I changed the subject. He listened.

"My daddy, the crazy one, used to tell us about these carnivorous cows in Tecum County. He said there was a whole herd of 'em. Long-haired cows. Brown, stringy, long-hair hangin' down like a wooly mammoth. He said they ate pigs. The farmer would throw a fat pig over the fence and those crazy-ass carnivorous cows would chase down the pig, stompin' and bitin', rippin' chunks of meat off the pig."

We just looked at each other a few seconds. I smiled first, and then he smiled, and then believe it or not, the doctor laughed. It was the first time I'd heard it. Round and full. Not loud, but a genuine, deep-down laugh.

There was a knock on the door behind the doctor. It swung open and a young jail guard told Dr. Andrews he had a telephone call in the docket room.

"Excuse me."

I took advantage of being alone again to look at the doctor's notes. The fresh notes were covered, probably on purpose, by a blank notepad. I squeezed my fingers under the crack between the screen and the metal table, barely able to reach the empty pad with my middle finger, pushing it a few inches to the side. I could read:

"I thought Danny was the smoker? Ask Joel. Addictions. *Remain detached."

It was a reminder to himself. Remain detached. The doctor's creed. If you become involved with the patient—sexually, intellectually, personally—it supposedly becomes impossible to analyze, evaluate, or treat the patient. You can't see them anymore. Or maybe you can see them too well.

Remain detached. Maybe this should be the creed of the human race. Remain detached, and you'll never have a reason to cry. Funerals would be solitary events, only the dead guy and the gravedigger. And, of course, the gravedigger would remain detached. Just another hole. Just another thing to do.

I looked at my hands. When I was fourteen years old

I dislocated the pinky finger on my right hand. We were playing basketball. I swiped at the ball, my pinky finger hit full force, the middle joint separated. I looked down to see the finger shaped like an L, pointing in a ninety-degree angle away from the other fingers. It was a strange thing to see.

One of the guys on the other team said his dad was a doctor. He said we needed to pull the finger back into place in five minutes or it would be permanently crooked, the ligaments freezing up and locking down. So I let him pull it. The pain was enormous. The kid turned his back to me, took hold of the injured finger, and pulled. And then he readjusted his grip, spread his feet apart, and pulled again with all his strength. The finger slid back where it belonged, but for the rest of my life it remained twice the size of the other pinky and hurts most of the time, especially when it's cold. It's rainy and cold now. Wintertime.

The door opened and the doctor came back into the room. I forgot to push the empty pad back over the fresh notes. The doctor looked down at the pad. He didn't say anything.

"Joel, the other day, when we were leaving, your mother asked about you needing cigarettes. In our earlier meetings, you told me about your brother Danny being the smoker. I've seen a pattern of you slipping in and out of your brother's identity, like the arrest for public intoxication in the train car."

A quick response didn't come to my mind, so I didn't answer at all.

"I've seen cases of people who become so empathetic, so sympathetic, with the plight of another person, they begin to see themselves in the skin of the other person. They literally experience, to some degree, inside their minds, the experiences of another person, life events they didn't experience in reality. They slide back and forth between themselves and the other person."

I wondered if the doctor would get to see his kids later that night. Maybe he was already ordered to weekends. Maybe he already had a second-floor apartment, unfurnished, just a mattress in the back bedroom, a refrigerator with nothing inside but a carton of milk and a half-eaten pizza.

"Danny rarely smoked. It was about the only addiction he didn't have."

"You didn't answer my question."

"It wasn't a question. He couldn't have just one drink, or take just one pain pill. Once he started, there was nothin' inside him to stop. He could watch the same porn movie a thousand times. I never could understand the pornography thing. It's an idiot's addiction. I mean, the sexual act is repetitious by nature. If you watch long enough the people become like dogs in the yard, humping each other, stuck together. That's the damnedest thing, isn't it? Dogs gettin' stuck together in the act of intercourse. If they decide they hate each other, it's too bad. It should happen that way to people."

"Why do you think Danny couldn't control his impulses?"

"Well, I've got this theory. There are three groups of people. All of us fall into one of the categories. There are certain people who will fuck up their lives no matter what. There are certain people who will succeed no matter what. And then there's everybody else, all those people who will fuck up or succeed depending on their place in this life, their parents, circumstances beyond their control. Victims, or beneficiaries, of the world.

"You see it everyday. A rich kid, great parents, opportunities unlimited, smokes cocaine, drinks himself to death. No one understands.

"Or the orphan, abandoned. Grows up in poverty, discrimination, violence. Pulls himself above it all. Earns an education, succeeds in business, ends up with a wonderful wife and perfect children.

"But if you don't fall in the first two categories, you

fall in the third. Not so weak to fail in the face of great potential, but not strong enough to rise above the badness of a world around you."

"Which category was Danny in?"

"He was in the first category. That's why I did what I did."

"What category are you in?"

"We don't know yet."

"Your answer shows optimism about having a future."

"I guess it does. I don't have Danny's blood. At least not the poison part. But I didn't know that until a few days ago."

For no obvious reason, I remembered the time I saw Danny downtown standing in front of the hardware store dressed like Jesus.

"One time, when Danny was about twenty years old, I saw my brother standing downtown in front of the hardware store dressed like Jesus. I was just driving past. He had long hair, a half-ass scraggly beard. He wore a robe and sandals and held a brown dog in his arm. The free arm was raised, palm to the sky.

"I didn't recognize him at first, driving by slow. It was the voice I recognized. Yelling over and over, 'May Abraham be with you. May Abraham be with you.'

"Why is it so many people with mental illness obsess on religion?"

"Did Danny obsess on religion?"

"Yeah, he did. He'd go through stages when he couldn't seem to think about anything else. He'd mix together bits and pieces of Christianity, mythology, science fiction, whatever seemed to fit in his private puzzle. He'd create a fundamental voodoo, but the commitment was absolute. Maybe faith is a sixth sense."

"Why have you reached your personal conclusions about religion?"

"Why? Why do you think? Those people who worship Jesus as the son of God don't give a crap about a long-haired, bearded man in front of the hardware store with his hand stretched out to the sky. They hate the people, the Jews, who failed to recognize Jesus as the son of God two thousand years ago, when they themselves, today, wouldn't recognize Jesus if they passed Him on the sidewalk. It's ridiculously hypocritical. If Jesus came back, He'd be in jail or a mental institution within twenty-four hours of His arrival. Maybe He'd get the shit beaten out of Him under a bridge by some rich college boys. Hell, maybe they'd crucify Him again.

"There are more atheists in church than anywhere else. They sit in the back, position themselves behind a

guy with a big head so they don't have to make eye contact with the preacher or the priest. They go to church to
be seen by their neighbors, or to feel better about their
odds of going to heaven, on the off chance heaven exists,
or to feel forgiven for cheating on their taxes or their
wives or the Saturday golf game. You don't absorb Christianity, you live it everyday."

"When did you begin to feel this way about religion?"

"My mother took us to church every Sunday. Maybe
it was just a chance to be away from the old man. Maybe
it was a chance for my mother to see the preacher.

"I never heard a word the preacher said. Don't you
think, if there was a God, He would have made me listen?
He would have kept me from sitting in the church lusting?
As a teenager, I spent half the time with an erection, imagining the ladies in the choir bent over the pew. What's
holy about that?

"Don't you think, if there was a God, He wouldn't
have just sat back and watched Danny cut himself, and
cry, and drink rubbing alcohol?"

"Maybe He didn't."

"What?"

"Maybe He didn't just sit back and watch."

I thought about what he said.

"Maybe you feel the way you do because you're angry at God."

I looked him in the face, a face that had become familiar. I couldn't really see the details anymore, just the faded outlines. Dr. Ellis Andrews was no longer a stranger. Maybe it changed when he laughed. Maybe when we spoke of his children. Maybe when he revealed his faith through his questions. I wondered how he saw me.

"Maybe so," I said. "After all, the only real secrets are the ones we keep from ourselves."

The doctor's eyes were so tired. He was slumped down in his chair noticeably. The world was pushing him down.

"I know you don't believe it now, but time heals. It's the only good piece of advice the crazy old man ever gave me. Time heals."

The doctor scratched the stubble on his chin. He looked at me hard with slightly sunken cheeks. I wished we were sitting at a coffee shop somewhere. A place, another kind of situation, where I could help him.

"The other night, when I was in bed, I couldn't sleep. I started to take kind of an inventory of my life. The only way you can measure your life is by the people who love you. I went through the list of my people.

"I'm not sure Danny was capable of love. There were times I think he loved me in a way I can't really understand, but it wasn't his fault. He did the best he could.

"The old man didn't love me. I know that for sure. And my real father didn't know me. It's easy to say you love something you don't know, but it isn't true, is it? It's not enough to love the idea of something. It's not enough to live at the end of the block and think of me down the street, in another man's house, all wrapped up in a lie. I don't think that's enough to call love.

"My mother's love was real, but it was so mixed together with need and guilt and dependence. Need isn't the same as love. She needed me to get through each day. If she loved me, how could she let that crazy son-of-a-bitch beat the shit out of me? How could she let me believe he was my father? She needed me to stay in that house with her. She needed me to be in the other room, in the dark, with my eyes wide open, listening. Part of who she was, her identity as a person, was protecting me and knowing, somehow, someday, I'd protect her. But it wasn't her fault anymore than Danny's. He was blood, and she was circumstance.

"Those mornings I told you about, when just me and Lisa were awake in the quiet house, I felt a love from her I've never felt from anyone else. She was too young to understand need. She was too innocent to pretend. She loved me. She would touch my face with those little hands, those little soft fingertips, and that's all there was.

That's all there needed to be. But of course, she doesn't exist, right? And I can't separate myself from my brother, right? And if you can't separate yourself from other people, and you believe in ghosts, how can you really figure out anything?"

"Let's go back to you and Danny. Do you admit it wasn't you in the train car?"

"How can I admit that? I was there. I saw it. I smelled it all over me. Your records are screwed up."

"Think about it. Think back. Did you pick Danny up at the police station? Did you smell the coal on him? Did you get it all over your hands when you changed his clothes?"

He was pushing me. Maybe I got too close with the personal comments. Remain detached. Remember what side of the metal screen you're on. Remember who's crazy and who's not. This is no coffeehouse. This is a jailhouse, and I shot my brother in the head. At least I thought it was my brother.

"There's something I didn't tell you."

"About what?"

"When I shot Danny. There's something I left out."

"What?"

"I had the gun to his head. I had it placed exactly where it needed to be. And Danny looked at me.

"I hesitated."

"You hesitated?"

"Yeah. Just for a second."

"Why did you leave that out before?"

"Don't you understand? I hesitated. I froze there for a second looking at him. If I thought it was right, if I was one hundred percent sure it was the right thing to do, why would I hesitate to pull the trigger?"

"Why do you think you hesitated?"

I stood up with my face against the cold screen. I put anger in my voice. "Stop fuckin' with me. You know why."

The doctor didn't flinch. There was confidence in the barrier between us. He just looked above the top of his glasses and said, "Say it."

I turned slowly around and walked to the far wall ten feet away. I stood and stared at the solid cinder block wall, my eyes unfocused, the details blurry. I concentrated until the texture of the cream-colored paint, the bumps in the cinder, were clear like a photograph. In the small channel between two blocks I saw a tiny black dot. It moved, and I watched it. A little black ant, the size of a period at the end of a sentence, moving slowly, stopping, and moving again, free to come and go as he wished. Free to find his way into jail, and free to find his way out again. I reached up with my index finger and smashed the little ant into oblivion. I didn't think about it, I just did it.

The doctor said, "Imagine the weakness of a heart never broken."

I didn't turn around.

"Imagine how fragile it would be, Joel, if we went through this life with no bruises, just kept our hearts buried inside our chests. We wouldn't be human."

I started to cry. My face tightened and my throat closed. I could feel it come up inside. It was the first time in a very long time, and it was out of my control. I just cried, my back to the doctor, the water in my eyes, the feeling of relief and embarrassment together.

And then it began to pass.

"Do you want to stop for the day?"

"No."

I wiped my eyes on my sleeve and turned around. The idea of going back to my cell wasn't a good one.

"I saw this story in the newspaper. A guy was sentenced to death. He stayed on death row for six years. There was an execution date on the calendar. About three months before he was scheduled to die, they cleared the guy with DNA testing. He didn't do it. He was convicted of raping and murdering a little girl, but he didn't do it.

"He was released from prison. Went home to what was left of his family. But you know what the guy did? He killed himself. He killed himself on the exact same day he was scheduled to be executed. He couldn't get past it. The date was burned in his mind. A certain day, in a certain month, on a certain calendar, marked in red, and he couldn't get past it."

We sat for a moment, quiet in the little room.

"I need to ask you some questions about the court system. Do you understand the role of the judge?"

"Yeah. He's the judge. He judges, makes sure everybody walks the line. Keeps his nose slightly in the air, keeps his robe buttoned tight, and plays God on occasion."

"What about the prosecutor?"

"His job is to convince the jury to convict me, and then convince the judge to do with me what he wants. And afterwards, give an interview to the TV station so his constituents won't vote him out of office and take away his government tit."

"The jury?"

"Twelve citizens, a jury of my peers, plucked from their daily routine, and asked to comprehend what they could not possibly comprehend, in a short period of time, with no training or experience, and then asked to make the most serious decision a person can make about another person's life, while drinking as much free coffee as possible."

"Your defense attorney?"

"A poorly dressed, appointed lawyer who couldn't make a living in private practice so he took an oath to help the downtrodden in between bad habits and bad golf. Mostly, he's just glad he isn't me, and I'm not him, and it's five o'clock, so let's go home and give this justice shit a rest."

"You've got a cynical view of our justice system."

"It's outdated and tired. We're still locking people away like medieval times. You should see the poor bastards in here. Half of them are crazy and crippled. The other half are uneducated, pissed-on leftovers, and nobody gives a flyin' shit whether they live or die."

"Which one are you?"

"A little bit of both, I guess, but I don't belong in here. Or maybe I do. It's hard to tell anymore. And by the way, what's your role in the criminal justice machine?"

"I test people, evaluate people, and submit a report to the court. Sometimes my recommendations are followed, and sometimes they're not."

"Does it make you mad when they don't follow your recommendations?"

"It can be frustrating."

"So people who don't have your qualifications, training, education, and years of experience in mental health can overrule you just because they want to?"

"I guess so."

"It doesn't seem right."

"No, it doesn't seem right, but then again, I'm just one man with one opinion."

"I guess if you tried hard enough you could find something wrong with everybody. You could diagnose everybody with some bullshit diagnosis. Prescribe a magic pill.

"If you fidget when you wait, or procrastinate, you've got Adult Attention Deficit Disorder. Take the yellow pill. If you get sad more than average, you're clinically depressed. Take the pink pill. Nobody's responsible for anything. It's just the illness."

"It's not that simple."

"Sure it is. People love categories. They want everything and everybody to fit neatly in a category. He's ADD. She's black. He's republican. Oh, I know that person. I know everything I need to know about them. I'm familiar with his category."

"People like to understand. Categories help make things seem more understandable. But truthfully, we are each our own category, unique and complicated. You're a perfect example, Joel. You're not your father. You're also not the man you thought was your father. You're not your mother, or your brother, or anyone else. You're just you. You have an identity outside of your situation."

"Do you think that's something I don't know? My father didn't help Danny. He just bailed him out of jail. My mother didn't do anything except pray. And Danny couldn't form the idea and hold it long enough to see a solution.

"Emerson wrote, 'It's as easy for the strong man to be strong as for the weak man to be weak.'

"Do you understand what that means? It's taken me a long time. Right and wrong have nothing to do with anyone else who has ever come before me. I won't inherit the shame, even if we all share the same blood down the line. There's a law within me, a law external to you. I'm not gonna beg."

The doctor thought a moment. The conversation was alive between us.

"On one hand, you talk about Emerson's 'Self-Reliance,' independence, living by your own set of rules. On the other hand, you talk about recognizing reality, like in the Walker Percy quote, 'Lucky is the man who does not secretly believe every possibility is open to him.' How do you reconcile those two philosophies?"

I smiled.

"I don't have to reconcile anything. I don't have to be consistent with anything I've ever said before. 'A foolish consistency is the hobgoblin of little minds.'

"It's the same as the categories. The consistency makes us feel safe. If we follow all the laws, rules, customs, and rituals of the past, surely everything will turn out O.K. Surely all those people couldn't be wrong.

"Well, they're wrong all the damn time. They were wrong when they thought the earth was flat, and wrong when they said cigarettes didn't cause cancer, and wrong when they thought it was a good idea for fifty-nine thousand Americans to die in Vietnam. Right?

"They were wrong when they came up with that bullshit, 'Separate but equal,' and when they nailed Jesus to the cross because they didn't like the new stuff he was talkin' about, and when they followed Hitler blindly and burned babies, one after another, ripped from their mother's arms. All in the name of consistency. Don't break ranks. As long as we follow what everyone else believes, we're not responsible individually when it goes wrong. It's somebody else's fault. Right?"

"How do the two philosophies, self-reliance and realism, fit with your idea that nothing matters?"

"Because in the end, it doesn't. In the end we're just a speck in the distance. Did you know most of the stars we see at night burned out thousands of years ago? What we see is the light that left them thousands of years earlier. Light traveling 186,000 miles every second, of every minute, of every hour, of every day, a thousand years before. Maybe millions of years before. And we see it like it's still there, a star in the galaxy, up there for us, like it gives a shit.

"Did you know that?"

"Yes. I've heard that before."

"Then you understand nothing matters. A realistic man grasps the concept that nothing matters. Nothing he has done, or will do, or could possibly do, will alter anything beyond the blink of his time and perhaps one blink more, like a particle of dust in the Pacific ocean.

"So the realistic man, who grasps and holds the reality that nothing matters, turns inward. He looks to himself for gratification in this life. To keep from losing all hope, to get himself out of bed in the morning, he creates his own reality. A reality where he is the king, and sets his own rules, and controls his own life on his own terms.

"It's the only way. Every great man in the history of

the world reached the same conclusion. Some of them didn't bother to figure out how they got to the conclusion. Instead, they invented, and conquered, and stepped outside other men's laws, and customs, and rituals. Emerson said, 'In every work of genius we recognize our own rejected thoughts: they come back to us with a certain alienated majesty.'

"You see what he's saying? We find in works of genius the ideas we rejected because they were our own. The very reason they should have been embraced. We turned the thoughts away because they weren't like all the old thoughts of a million other men before."

"Have you ever written down these ideas?"

"I could take a hundred pages to explain it, but all I'd be doing is saying the same thing a hundred different ways. You either get it or you don't, and I think you get it.

"Doctor, once you realize nothing matters, then you're free to do the right thing. You're free to do what's right for me."

It was the invisible line between us, asking for his help. I knew it could go several different directions, but I was running out of time.

"Joel, do you remember the first time we met, you told me you needed your eyeglasses? Do you remember that?"

I pretended to think about it.

"I remember."

"Your mother says you don't wear glasses. She says your brother wore glasses since he was six years old."

I didn't answer.

"Is that true?"

"Danny was supposed to wear his glasses, but most of the time he didn't. He was always coming up with some crazy idea to cure his vision. One week he ate nothing but carrots. Carrots for breakfast, carrots for lunch, carrots for supper. Another time he spent three or four nights lying on the roof looking up at the moon. He thought the silver particles from the moon would enter his eyes and take away the blur. He ended up with mosquito bites all over his forehead."

"Did you lie to me?"

"What?"

"Did you lie to me when you said you needed your glasses?"

"No."

The doctor scribbled on his notepad, but like before, he held the pad at a tilt so I couldn't steal the words.

"Now that you know about your real father, has it changed the way you feel about your mother?"

It was a good question, but I was having a hard time leaving the last subject behind. The glasses. For some reason I kept seeing myself at the kitchen table of our house wearing glasses. I could see it like a dream. The newspaper. A coffee cup.

When we dream, it seems odd we see ourselves from a distance, a perspective we can never have in the real world. Were Danny's dreams blurry, or did his subconscious correct his eyesight the way the carrots and moon particles failed to do? Were the glasses I wore at the kitchen table Danny's glasses, or was it just a stupid dream?

"Not really," I said.

"We've talked about how religious obsession is sometimes a characteristic of mental illness. Do you think your rebellion against established religion could be a sign of a problem?"

"I don't know. I never thought about it like that. It's just the idea of God doesn't fit. If time and space are infinite, and nothing we can do really matters, why would God put us in such a place? And if we're required to recognize the bleak reality to survive, and then take the next step to self-reliance, where is God in all that? I'm not a devil worshiper. I'm a realist.

"I read a story in the newspaper. A twenty-one-year-old guy in jail in Sherman, Texas, was arrested for cutting out the hearts of his ex-wife and daughter. He tore out his eye with his bare hands in his jail cell and quoted the verse Mark 9:47: 'And if your eye causes you to sin, pluck it out. It is better for you to enter the kingdom of God with one eye than to have two eyes and be thrown into hell.'

"Now that's some crazy shit. He thought his eyeball made him do it, so he ripped it out of his head and held it in his hand.

"I saw a ghost once."

"A ghost? What kind of ghost?"

"I was probably ten years old, maybe eleven. I woke up in the middle of the night. There was a man standing in the doorway to my room. He was some kind of soldier.

"I watched him, afraid to move, and he watched me, just standing there. I knew it was a ghost because when he left, he didn't turn and walk away, he just disappeared. Just faded slowly over a period of a few minutes until the outside was gone.

"I've never told anybody that before."

"Maybe you're looking at it upside down. Maybe you don't find a place for God to fit inside your life. Maybe you find a place for your life to fit inside God."

"I guess that depends on where you put the burden. Is it my job to prove He exists, or is it His job to show himself?"

I didn't want to go too far. Dr. Andrews seemed

unsteady. It wasn't the time to question his faith. He checked his watch and then looked directly at me to see if I noticed. I just smiled.

"This is our last session, Joel. I'll come by and see you late next week with a copy of the completed evaluation. We'll talk about it before it's filed with the court."

I was almost alone again. We sat and looked at each other for a long disconnected moment. I just waited.

"There are some things I want you to do. I want you to draw, Joel. I'll write a letter to the chief jailer asking him to make sure you've got access to the library. I'll drop off some good paper and pencils.

"And grow a beard. Have you ever had a beard before?"
    "No."

"Let it grow. It's wintertime. You're not the same person you thought you were a few weeks ago. Look different in the mirror.

    "And try to imagine what you would do, where you would go, if you left this place. Let your mind wander outside the walls. Expect the worst, but be prepared for the best. You've got to allow yourself some hope."

    "I don't understand."

"Why do you always have to understand everything, Joel?"

I watched him gather up his papers and followed his hands imagining myself organizing each item into a system, and then lining up the pages neatly on top of one another before they're closed away in the brown binder.

I felt a quiet anxiety, like the air was leaving the room but there wasn't anything I could do about it. I tried to think about what the doctor said. Paper and pencils, a beard, and places outside the walls of the jail, outside the walls built around me.

"Hey, don't do anything crazy."

"Like what?"

"I don't know. Get real drunk. Try to go see your wife at two o'clock in the morning. Get arrested. End up in here."

He barely smiled.

"Don't worry, Joel. I don't do stuff like that."

"I know. That's what's got me worried."

He stood at the door. He seemed to have a moment of hesitation. A moment of fear about what lies outside. But he said, "I'll see you next week," and opened the door anyway.

My face itched. It was a weird feeling, like something was stuck to my cheeks. My beard was only ten days old, and not really a beard yet, but I liked it anyway. It came out dark red, the whiskers I mean. I wondered if John Clayton grew dark red whiskers.

I felt better. The time in the library was good. Away from everybody. I could spend hours at the table with my pens and paper, forgetting where I was, or even who I was. There were times I would look up and not remember anything for a few seconds. Those few seconds were like gold.

Access to the library also gave me a little extra freedom. I was able to walk down once-forbidden hallways, past the kitchen, past storage rooms, stairways. It doesn't seem like much, but any flash of light to a blind man is a small miracle.

The doctor was late. I sat in my familiar chair touching my tongue to the mustache whiskers above my lip. They were sharp and hard, a strange place for whiskers to grow at all. Why could we possibly need hair on our lips? How could such a thing help me survive in the wild?

The door opened and in walked Dr. Andrews. He seemed hurried, but I could tell he purposefully slowed his movements immediately so he wouldn't appear in a hurry. He sat down.

"Good morning."

"Good morning."

"I like your beard. You look different."

"It's kinda half-ass, but I like it myself."

The doctor pulled out the typed and stapled report. He set the binder down on the floor.

"This is the evaluation, Joel. I want you to take a few minutes to read it. I've got to talk with a man down the hall. I'll be back."

The doctor slid the report under the metal screen. I was a little afraid to take it, and when I touched the paper, and pulled toward me, it seemed the doctor was a little afraid to let it go.

He got up and left the room.

ELLIS L. ANDREWS, PhD, ABPS
Diplomate Clinical Forensic Psychology
American Board Psychological Specialities

FORENSIC EVALUATION REPORT

NAME: Joel Stabler

AGE: Twenty-nine years

SEX: Male

RACE: Caucasian

FILE NO.:   0049430

TESTS ADMINISTERED: Wechsler Adult Intelligence Scale, Wide Range Achievement Test, Bender-Gestalt, Multi-phasic Personality Inventory, and Competency to Stand Trial Assessment.

REFERRAL INFORMATION

Joel Stabler was referred for evaluation by the Circuit Court. He was to undergo testing and evaluation for Competency to Stand Trial and Mental State at the Time of the Offense. The subject has been charged with the murder of his brother.

NOTIFICATION

Prior to beginning the evaluation, the Defendant was informed of the purpose and limited confidentiality of the information to be obtained. He was told a written report would be submitted to the Court, with copies made available to his attorney and the District Attorney. He was also informed that the written report or testimony by the examiner may be used in court proceedings to help determine Competency to Stand Trial and Mental State at the Time of the Alleged Offense, but none of the information would be used as evidence against him concerning guilt or innocence of the charges. The Defendant indicated he understood the purpose and limited confidentiality of the evaluation and agreed to proceed.

SUMMARY OF ALLEGED OFFENSE

According to the District Attorney's Office, the subject allegedly shot his brother in the head and then called police. There was no apparent motive, and the Defendant gave no statement to police. It should be noted the brother apparently suffered a lifetime of severe mental illness with frequent hospitalization, suicide attempts, drug and alcohol abuse, self-mutilation, incarceration, and delusions.

BACKGROUND INFORMATION

Information was provided by the subject and his mother. The mother became pregnant with Joel at sixteen years of age during an affair with a married preacher. Unwilling to pursue the relationship with the natural father, the mother married an older man by the name of Emmitt Stabler. Mr. Stabler provided necessities of a homeplace and food but apparently suffered from schizophrenia and alcoholism. Emmitt Stabler fathered Joel's brother, Daniel, and according to Joel's mother, believed he was the natural father of Joel also. Joel Stabler himself did not learn the truth of his natural father until the information was revealed through this evaluation.

The subject was physically and mentally abused by Mr. Stabler. Joel's physical development was normal, walking at eleven months and toilet-trained by his second birthday. However, due to the violence and instability inside the family homeplace, Joel began at an early age to assume the role of protector for his mother and younger brother. He suffered severe separation anxiety when forced to begin attending school.

Joel's fine and gross motor skills were above average, and there were no problems with his hearing or eyesight. There was no history of asthma, allergies, or diabetes. Joel has a poor sleeping routine, perhaps linked to fears from his childhood.

Joel has maintained employment his entire adult life and attended one year of college. He has never been married or had children of his own, unable to make such commitments primarily due to his overwhelming sense of obligation and responsibility to his mother and brother. The subject has few, if any, close friends.

BEHAVIORAL OBSERVATIONS

The subject is cooperative. It should be noted the test results reveal a high level of intelligence. Although cooperative, Joel is also guarded and careful with his responses. He is highly observant.

There were occasional mood swings, and on at least one occasion the subject suffered some type of physical episode, unable to catch his breath. The conversation was lively, with the subject sometimes speaking rapidly, jumping from one topic to the next. He bites his fingernails out of habit instead of obvious anxiety.

The subject demonstrated a need to control the session, undoubtedly a reaction to his lack of control over his child-hood homeplace and the abuse suffered at the hands of Emmitt Stabler.

Joel has no verifiable criminal history, no known psychi-atric diagnosis, and no apparent substance dependence. It should be noted that throughout the evaluation Joel Stabler attributed to himself characteristics of his brother, and vice-versa, unable at times to separate completely the two people. The subject also repeatedly spoke of a non-existent little sister named Lisa who apparently died at birth. It is the opinion of the examiner that these delusions are actual and not contrived by the subject.

TEST RESULTS

1. **Intelligence**:

On the WAIS-III Joel scored 184 (IQ) placing him in the top 1st percentile when compared with adults in his age category. There was a 95% probability that his actual intelligence would lie somewhere between IQ 178 and IQ 189.

Verbal Score	182
Performance Score	192
Full Scale Score	184
Verbal Comprehension	184
Perceptual Organization	191

On the WRAT-3 Joel scored well above average in reading identification skills and basic mathematical computation. His spelling skills were average.

2. **Neurological Screening**:

There were no distortions on the Bender-Gestalt suggestive of diffuse brain damage.

3. **Personality**:

On the MMPI-2, Joel's responses indicated a haphazard recognition of social boundaries. He tends to internalize for self-preservation, sometimes seemingly unaware of how he may appear to other people, and other times acutely aware of his predicament.

The line between reality and fantasy has been crossed so many times inside his mind, there is virtually no line at all in some areas. He can be defensive or aggressive, and in the next moment vulnerable like a child.

The subject is overly aware of his environment, perhaps due to a natural curiosity and intelligence, but also a result of years protecting himself and his family from attacks by Emmitt Stabler. Like an animal, he has grown highly sensitive to his surroundings. As Joel is a part of his own environment, he studies himself intently, seeking understanding. In between rational thinking patterns, the subject shows indications of psychosis.

FORENSIC ASSESSMENT

1.   **Competency to Stand Trial:**

On the Competency to Stand Trial Assessment Instrument and the Georgia Court Competency Instrument Joel demonstrated strong understanding of the criminal charge against him as well as the range and nature of possible penalties. He had no problem identifying court personnel and their roles in the process. His opinion of the American Judicial System is cynical, and he reveals little hope of a fair outcome.

The subject's capacity to disclose to his attorney pertinent facts is more than adequate. He is capable of assisting in planning a legal strategy or weighing the choices of a plea bargain agreement; however, the examiner holds serious doubts the Defendant could testify on his own behalf effectively due to factors outlined in following portions of this report.

2. **Mental State at the Time of the Offense:**

The Defendant was questioned extensively regarding his childhood, family dynamics, memory of the death of his brother, motivations, and other details. He has a vivid memory and many aspects of his recollections were verified by his mother as well as outside sources.

For his entire life, Joel Stabler has lived under the weight of mental illness. He was physically abused and mentally tortured, both intentionally and unintentionally, by the schizophrenic man he believed to be his father. As a small child Joel recognized his role as the protector of his mother as well as his younger brother. Unfortunately, the younger brother began to show unmistakable signs of the ravages of mental illness at a young age and Joel was ingrained with the idea his own mental health was destined to deteriorate based upon the belief he carried the same genes as the father and brother. It was just a matter of time.

Being blessed, or cursed, with such a strong mind, Joel Stabler essentially created his own destructive destiny. To survive in such a difficult environment, Joel constructed delusions. He invented a little sister, Lisa, who could be the embodiment of hope in a hopeless situation. He sharpened the ability to empathize to such a degree he blurred the lines between himself and his brother until it literally became difficult to see the difference.

The phenomenon can be described as a reverse placebo

effect. Instead of the human mind healing through positive belief, Joel's mind effectively made him mentally ill. He caused his own mental illness, as real as a chemical imbalance in the brain, as real as the schizophrenia suffered by his brother and the man who he believed to be his father. To some degree, the revelation of his real natural father has set Joel free. To another degree, it has opened up great avenues of unanswered questions about his identity as a person.

The term "psychosomatic" is defined as one who evidences bodily symptoms or bodily and mental symptoms as a result of a moral conflict. Joel Stabler is psychosomatic. The term "psychological moment" is defined as the occasion when the mental atmosphere is most certain to be favorable to the full effect of an action or event. Joel Stabler, under extreme conditions, psychosomatic, reached a psychological moment, a moral conflict, where he truly believed killing his brother was the right, and the only, thing to do. His temporary insanity was the result of circumstances, and he did not, and could not, have known his actions were wrong. It is the opinion of the examiner that Joel Stabler is not criminally responsible for the death of his brother.

SUMMARY AND CONCLUSIONS

The evaluation of the Defendant is complete. In my years as a clinical forensic psychologist, Joel is one of the most complicated and interesting legally sane individuals I have ever examined. My findings indicate the subject has adequate factual knowledge of the courtroom procedure and is competent to stand trial if necessary. My findings also indicate Joel Stabler is a highly intelligent individual who endured remarkably difficult life circumstances and found himself in a psychological moment, inside a complex moral dilemma, resulting in a man taking action he believed necessary, correct, and humane, to protect and free his brother.

The opinions expressed in this report are advisory only. As a clinical forensic psychologist, I recognize and respect that decisions regarding an individual's Competence and Mental State should be made by a judge or jury.

Ellis L. Andrews, PhD, ABPS
Clinical Forensic Psychologist

It's strange to see my entire life condensed in a few pages. I read the report, and then read it again. At one point I saw the doctor peek through the small square window on the door, but I didn't look up, and he went away again.

When I see things in black and white, the written words on pages we can hold in our hands, they seem much more real. How could I have such clear memories of

Lisa, of being in the coal car? What parts of my other memories were imagined, and what parts really happened? And most of all, how could the doctor tell the difference if I can't?

It was raining outside. A cold February rain. I saw it from the thin window in my cell, but I couldn't hear it in the meeting room. I had to imagine the gray sky, seamless, moving west to east, the cold steady rain falling through the pine trees, dripping to the brown flat grass below. I don't remember Lisa anywhere except in the house, in her room, or alone with me in the kitchen in the morning. I don't remember her at the pine tree place, or at the supper table, or in the front yard, or anywhere else. Her face looking up in the cold rain, eyes tight shut, light mist in the lashes, hands in the pockets of her jacket. Complete freedom.

The doctor came back in the room. He sat down and leaned over to pick up the binder on the floor.

"Do you have any questions about the report?"

"Have you ever heard of cross-sensualization?"

"I don't think I have."

"It's a person's ability to taste what they see, hear what they feel. The senses are rewired, crossed over from one to the other. You can actually taste in your mouth something you can see across the room, you can smell the smoke from a fire on television, actually close your eyes and see the train you can hear a mile away around a corner. Do you believe in such a thing?"

"I don't know. I've never heard of it before. It sounds like it would be hard to figure out what was real and what wasn't."

"What do people call you, Eli or Ellis?"

"Mostly Ellis. My mother called me Eli."

"Is she still alive?"

There was a moment of hesitation to answer. Small, almost undetectable hesitation, but still there. The old fear of crossing the line of detachment. I'm not the only one cautious and guarded.

"No."

"Do you think I have little blue jelly balls floating in my veins?"

"No, I don't."

I thought about it. I could still see them, bright blue, tiny to the naked eye, huge under a microscope, floating through my veins like beach balls on a raging river, bouncing against each other, occasionally bursting, blue jelly oozing into the red river, the membrane exterior disappearing under the bubbling rapids.

"Do you have any questions about the report, Joel?"

"Yeah. At one point you say I'm not criminally responsible because of temporary insanity. Later you call me legally sane."

"The distinction is time. I think at the time you killed Daniel, you weren't criminally responsible under the definition in the law. I think now, as we sit here right now, you're perfectly sane, you're competent under the definition of competent under the law."

"So I can't be found guilty of murdering my brother?"

"In my opinion, no. But you have to know, Joel, my report probably won't make any difference at all. They'll just get another doctor to say something different. The judge and the District Attorney have to run for office. They're politicians. This is a conservative county. They can't appear weak. You killed a man. You shot a man in the head, and you're not foaming at the mouth or rolling around on the ground eating your own feces. Temporary insanity isn't exactly a popular defense among voters."

The doctor was apologetic and defensive at the same time. He was part of a system that sometimes failed, but he was still part of the system. I did notice a sadness in his face. A sadness meant for me, like I was the last straw and he couldn't fake it anymore.

"It doesn't matter anyway. Remember when I told you time heals, time heals all wounds. It's not true. For some things, there just isn't enough time. Maybe they would eventually heal, but there just aren't enough years left to put between yourself and the bad thing.

"If we care to look, everybody has a day when their mortality is clear. We will die. No matter how hardworking, moral, intelligent, honest, you can't buy yourself one more single day with any of it. There are no exceptions to the rule. It's just a matter of making it to the next spring, because there will be a year when each of us won't. Nobody has clean hands.

"Did you ever hear a song by John Prine called *The Great Compromise*?"

"No."

"Sometimes, without really knowing it, or making a purposeful decision, through years of gradual movement in the same direction, we reach a point where we realize we've compromised ourselves too far. We can't do what's right anymore, because we can't know what's right. We've given ourselves away, and never really noticed."

Dr. Andrews was silent, but the silence was filled with something. He was on the edge, and any sound, any movement, could affect the balance. He floated like a feather waiting for a breeze and then floated quietly to rest.

Finally, he said, "I've been coming here, to this jail, a long time. I sit in this room and talk to people about their lives. Sometimes it takes a while for the guards to get the inmate from his cell. Sometimes I sit in here alone and think. I think about how I'd escape. I've lain awake in bed at night thinking about it. I don't know why. It's just something I think about."

As I've said before, when you've spent your whole life waiting for the craziness to come, you can't be sure which strange idea, which suspicious thought, will be the one to start the slide into dementia. Was the doctor saying what I thought he was saying? I waited.

"You know how I'd do it? A new grand jury is empaneled every two months. Eighteen people selected at random from the jury pool. They don't know each other. By law, the grand jury has to inspect the county jail, make sure the conditions are humane, whatever. They're given a tour, and usually the tour is given the first day they're empaneled. In other words, eighteen people, who don't know each other, who aren't known by the jail guards, walk through here once every two months.

"It would be easy to blend in. There's no head count. There's no identification check. This isn't a maximum security prison, it's a county jail."

It was obvious he'd really thought about it a long time. He spoke the words as though he'd said them to himself before. Like he was tempted to write them down, but wouldn't dare, in case they were found, and someone would misunderstand, like having a mistress.

What other vivid games were played inside the doctor's mind? What other improper thoughts did he hold? I listened.

"If a man was to change his appearance, maybe shave off a beard people had gotten used to, cut his hair, wear glasses. If a man was to get his hands on a shirt, a pair of pants, some shoes, maybe from a storage room on the way to the library, accidentally left unlocked by a trustee, a storage room with all the inmates' clothes they wore when arrested, he could become part of the crowd, become the nineteenth juror on the tour, and simply walk out the front door. When he got to the courthouse, he could excuse himself to the bathroom and just disappear."

As I listened, it occurred to me I'd been in jail for months and never once thought of escape. My mind had spent every minute turned in a different direction, but now there was something new to think about.

"On February 23rd, after lunch, the next grand jury will come through here."

"I've been thinking about what you said. About God's place. About where faith fits. I haven't finished thinking about it yet."

"I won't be coming back to see you, Joel. If we see each other again, it'll probably be in a courtroom."

I hadn't noticed before, but Dr. Andrews was wearing his wedding band again. He saw me look, and there was no need to say anything. No need at all.

He reached his hand up, the left hand, and removed his eyeglasses. He folded them together slowly, lowered his hand to the stainless steel table top, and gently slid the glasses under the metal screen to my side.

"Good luck to you, Joel," he said, and I watched him pick up his brown binder and walk away from me for the last time.

Dr. Ellis L. Andrews
(Friday, March 25th)

Joel escaped from the county jail on February 23rd. It was front page news: Murderer on the Loose. Besides his mother, I was probably the only one who smiled when I heard about it. Maybe we smiled for different reasons.

The chief jailer was crucified by the press. How could a murderer just walk out the front door of the jail? When they figured out he escaped, schools were locked down, roadblocks were set up, and Joel Stabler was long gone. At first they were looking for a long-haired man with a reddish beard wearing an orange jumpsuit instead of a clean shaven, short-haired guy with glasses, khaki slacks, loafers, and a blue windbreaker. A trustee must have accidentally left the storage room near the library unlocked. The eighteen strangers must not have noticed the nineteenth stranger fall in line near the door to the kitchen. And then where was Joel Stabler? Not in his bed. Not in the meeting room with his lawyer or doctor. Not sitting in the library lost in a faraway place. He was gone.

There were rumors and alleged sightings. At first, nobody had any idea how he pulled it off. They went through the hours of videotape and pieced it together. That's when they changed the face on television, no long hair or reddish beard, but instead, a clean-cut guy with a nice pair of glasses. Of course, there is no video camera in the meeting room of the jail. Communications with doctors and lawyers are privileged and protected.

I received a telephone call from Joel's mother two days later. She said, "They follow me when I go to the store. They sit outside my home and act like they're invisible. Are they stupid? Do they think Joel would come here?"

"They've got to do what they can. I'm sure they've tapped your phone. They'll check your mail," I told her.

"Can they do that?" she asked.

"I'm not a lawyer, but I think so."

I ended the conversation as soon as possible without being rude. The next morning, the investigators from the District Attorney's Office showed up at my office door. I had met both of them before, a fat guy named Frank Wilkes and a young guy, maybe twenty-five years old, named Andy Carthidge. The young guy, when he stepped into my office, held a copy of Joel's written psychological evaluation in his hand.

The big guy sat down and said, "Doc, you wouldn't happen to know where we could find Joel Stabler?"

The young one was pacing around my office. He looked like he hadn't slept in days, caffeine and testosterone keeping him going strong.

"I don't have any idea, Frank. He never said anything to me about planning an escape."

Frank Wilkes stuck out his puffy hand and Andy Carthidge placed the report between his fingers.

"I've read this report here, Doc, and I'll be damned if I can make heads or tails of it. Is the guy nuts or not?"

"It's not as simple as that, but to answer your question, no, I don't think he's nuts anymore."

The young one had his hands on his hips with his head tilted slightly to the side like I was speaking Portuguese.

Frank leaned his heavy body forward in the chair and said, "If you had to guess, would you say he'd be inclined to seek revenge, or blow off his own head, or go to Mexico and live in a pueblo eatin' beans and tortillas?"

"He's a smart man, Frank, but his whole life's been spent in this county. I'm not sure he'd do very well on the run in a place like Mexico. If I had to guess, I'd say he's still around here. And no, I don't think he'd seek revenge or hurt anybody, including himself. I suppose if he did commit suicide, it would solve your problem."

Andy Carthidge said, "He better hurry up, because when I see the son-of-a-bitch I'm gonna blow his brains out."

Frank looked up at the young man, and then turned back to me.

"Doc, if you hear anything, I'm sure you'll let us know. And by the way, did you write a letter to the chief jailer asking permission for Stabler to use the library?"

I felt myself swallow.

"I did."

"Why?" he asked.

I tried very hard not to swallow again.

"I felt like he needed time away from the other inmates. I felt like he needed a chance to have an outlet."

Andy Carthidge said, "He found an outlet alright."

Frank Wilkes studied me for a long time. Finally the big man's frame rose from the chair, and the two left me alone in the office. I paid particular attention over the next day or two, but I was sure I wasn't being followed.

After Joel was gone a week, it was still front page news, but mostly there was nothing new to report. The chief jailer resigned his position. Frank Wilkes gave the same quote over and over, "We'll get him. It's just a matter of time."

On a Saturday morning I found myself driving down Highway 49 on my way to the river. It occurred to me I was near Joel's pine tree place. I stopped where he told me to stop and walked down the edge of the empty cotton field. Above the tree line of the woods I could see the tops of several pine trees towering over the others. It was a beautiful day, the sky a rich blue, with a few billowing clouds floating across the horizon.

As I got closer, I felt anxiety. Was it possible Joel would be standing in the place he described? Would I step around a corner in the path and see him in the columns of light?

He wasn't there. I stood in the circle of the big tree trunks. I placed my hand against one and pushed, just to feel the complete resistance, the massive strength. The quiet had an ownership, a hold over the space, like no sounds could enter through invisible walls. I just stood and listened, closing my eyes and tilting my face upwards to Heaven, and the tops of the mighty pine trees, and the sky. I expected to hear the sound of feet on the path, leaves under the weight of a shoe, the snap of a small gray stick. But there was nobody.

On an oak tree, near the outer circle of pines, I found a place where the bark had been removed. Carved in the wood it said: Joel and Danny were here. I could feel their presence. I could hear their voices. They had been there, and in many ways would be there forever, like the majestic giant pines reaching to the clouds.

On the morning of March 23rd, my phone rang. Joel Stabler was found dead of natural causes in a farmhouse in Montana. He died one day after his thirtieth birthday, apparently of the same congenital heart defect that killed his natural father at the same age. His mother cried on the telephone, and I listened while she cried. She was the last one left, the beginning and the end.

We're sympathetic, and then it's time to eat. We're overcome with sadness for another, and then we fall asleep. Cancer, suicide, heart attacks, car wrecks, shootings, are just the way of the world. We pretend we're shocked, but we're not. Deep inside, no matter how buried we are in comforts and stability, we know the world is a dangerous and unpredictable place to be.

Joel was freed of the bonds of one man's blood, only to feel the constraints of another. They said he died in his sleep in a little house where he stayed on a farm. I expect Joel felt lost on the run, not able to go home. On the same day I got the phone call, a fat envelope arrived in the mail with a Montana postmark.

Dr. Andrews:

I'm in Montana, the big country. It's a beautiful place, cold and golden as far as a man can see. Lots of room to think. I got a job working on a farm, hard work, up early in the morning, tired by sunset. Believe it or not, this is the best I've slept my whole life. I never knew what it felt like to wake up in the morning rested. Who would think I'd get my best sleep on the run, a fugitive from justice? I'm rested, but at the same time, a little lost. It's that magic feeling of nowhere to go.

I miss my mother very much. You asked me if finding out about my real father, and the decisions of my mother, changed the way I feel about my mother. The answer is 'no.' How I feel about her has been a constant in my life, maybe the only constant, since the day I came to this world. I wish my child could feel that way about me, but it's hard now to envision my future, especially with a baby. I would be a good father, though. Strict, but not too strict. I would always keep my promises, and walk the line between setting a strong example and never forgetting what it was like to be a child. I would wake up in the morning and remind myself each day of the choice I made. My child over alcohol. My child over skipping work on a rainy day. My child over shiny cars, laziness, suicide, freedom, pornography, guns, gambling, and whatever else needs to go. And then I'd walk to my little boy's room and look at him while he slept. Look at his face. It's not a sac-

rifice. Tell my mother I love her. Tell her there are
still a few dreams left to catch.

I've sent along some drawings. My mind is
pure again with the lines. I see something beautiful in every direction. Danny is with me. If it's
true, like you say, I began to blur the lines
between myself and my brother, then in a way
Danny is still alive, with me, in this farmhouse in
Montana. I've noticed the bad memories beginning to fade. Maybe there won't be anything left
but good. I can see him fishing. Not on that last
day, but on all the days before. The days the fish
were biting, and the sun was hot, and Danny
would laugh at stupid things. The only fear with
forgetting the bad memories is the fear I will
wake up one day and not remember why I did
what I did. I can't have it both ways.

So how much of who I am comes from
Emmitt Stabler, and how much comes from John
Clayton? The age-old ultimate question with a
few original twists and turns. Who exactly am I?
Over the last month it's become clearer with each
passing day. The hard work, the time alone, the
quiet. Drawing imaginary women in fields of
grain. Maybe not so imaginary at all. Before, there
was always someone else to put ahead of myself.

Now I'm first in line. I have John Clayton's patience, Emmitt Stabler's capacity for violence, my mother's love, Danny's fear, and Lisa's wide-open arms. I have the old man's temper, my mother's instinct to protect, Danny's disconnection, and my father's faith. Good or bad, these are the things I have.

Today would be a good day to die. I don't mean that in a bad way. It's my thirtieth birthday, March 20th, the first day of spring. I woke up last night in the middle of the night and it came to me clear. You know how that happens sometimes? You're too tired to write it down, so in a half-lucid dream state you swear to remember, but the next morning you're lucky if you remember there was something you should have remembered. This time I wrote it down. It was too clear, and too important, to let go.

A child is born.

Over time, if he is able, it is inevitable he will recognize the reality of the apparent insignificance of his existence. It cannot be ignored by the capable.

At this point of recognition, most people believe man comes to a fork in the road. Go left and turn inward for solace and satisfaction: self-reliance. Go right and turn to the idea of a higher power for understanding and relief: faith in God. This is incorrect. There is another choice, a third road in between, not left nor right: self-realism.

Turning inward is not turning away from faith. Turning to faith is not turning away from self. They are the same. How else to explain the stars? The road to the left will eventually lead to disappointment. The road to the right will lead to belief in nothing. Some people, most people, don't recognize the futility in the first place. They are either simply incapable of the recognition, or they subconsciously refuse to see it. They divert themselves with work, children, lust, alcohol, the quest for money or power. They don't see it because they don't want to see it. But ignorance isn't really bliss, it's just ignorance.

Of the people who do truly recognize the futility, many can't, or don't, take the next step. They just stay in the abyss, unable to live with any purpose. These are often the ones who kill themselves or turn into bitter, lonely old people waiting for the relief they believe death will bring.

Of the people who do recognize the futility, and do take the next step to exploring, the vast majority either choose the safe road to religion or the paved road to self-reliance. Very few make the long difficult trip to the land of everything. Very few possess the fortitude to recognize, the strength to proceed, the wisdom to pass the fool's gold, and the endurance to prevail. Very few. But these few are the true leaders of the human race. They are the people who set the direction of history and move us all forward into the future.

We are God, and God is us, and the lines between have blurred until there are no lines at all. Nothing else can bring a man peace. Nothing.

Joel

Joel's body was brought home. The funeral was on a Saturday morning. I decided to go to the graveside service. I kept telling myself it wasn't a good idea, but I went anyway. If he hadn't sent me the letter, maybe I wouldn't have gone.

The narrow road through the cemetery circled back around until I reached a group of cars. Fifty yards away I could see a handful of people, mostly in black, standing in the cold gray day. There was a light mist falling, and I anticipated the coldness I would feel walking to the grave, but I opened the car door anyway, and headed down the hill. The grass was brown and hard under my shoes. The headstones had names like Morris and Weeks, Monroe and Collier.

As I got closer, I could hear the preacher speaking. He'd already started the service. I stood in my overcoat behind the others. I didn't see anybody from the newspaper or television. I didn't see any police. The story was old. The case was closed. Joel's mother turned her head to see me. She smiled awkwardly and turned away. Next to her was a blonde girl, maybe eighteen or nineteen years old. She looked at me. I nodded politely, and the young woman turned back to the preacher. I couldn't stop looking at the back of her head. I could feel my heart beat inside my chest. "It must be a family friend, or a cousin, maybe somebody from out of town," I thought. I tried to level my breathing and listen to the words of the man talking about a person he probably never knew. My hands were clinched in the bottoms of the pockets of my new overcoat. The cold was up inside my bones. I could see the breath of the preacher.

"And God forgives us our sins," he was saying.

I stopped listening and counted. Lisa was born when Joel was twelve. She'd be eighteen years old. I counted again. Only ten people, including myself and the preacher. Only eight other people in the entire world cared enough to come to the man's funeral. How many of those eight only showed up out of obligation to the mother, relatives, or church members?

I leaned a little to my left. The blonde girl was holding

the hand of Joel's mother. Holding tight. "It couldn't be," I thought to myself. "It couldn't be Lisa. There is no Lisa." I tried to listen again. Joel's mother was the only person crying.

"Ashes to ashes, dust to dust," the man said.

In a few minutes it was over. It was too cold to stand around and make small talk. It didn't feel much like spring. Everybody started to walk to their cars, so I started too, hands still in my pockets, face against the wind. When I got to my car I looked back down the hill to the grave. The blonde girl was standing alone. I touched my hand to the doorhandle and stopped. Sometimes it's better not to know. Sometimes it's better to drive away, but I couldn't do it. I couldn't drive away this time.

So I turned around and walked back down the hill, counting my steps out of habit. Joel's grave was next to Danny's and Danny's grave was next to Emmitt Stabler. The girl stood alone, looking down at the headstone of Daniel Allen Stabler. I made myself take the last two steps until I stood next to her. She didn't look at me. We were quiet for a time.

"I'm Ellis Andrews."

"I know," she said.

We were quiet again. The gravestone read, "Daniel Allen Stabler—loving son and brother—it's time to rest."

The girl said, "You're the doctor who wrote the report

I saw on my mother's kitchen table."

She looked up at me. "I'm Lisa."

Before I could think I said, "Your mother told me you didn't exist. I don't understand."

The girl laughed. The laugh was soft, lost in the air, almost like she was laughing to herself. "From your report it looks like you never quite figured it out."

"Figured out what?" I asked.

I leaned closer to her. She said, "It doesn't really matter anymore, does it?"

It was another chance to walk away. I thought of Joel. I thought of the drawings he sent from Montana. Beautiful, like he was seeing something I couldn't see, in a simple face or a tree or a wide open field stretching to a mountain far away.

"It matters to me," I said.

"Are you sure you really want to know? You can go back to your warm office, have a cup of coffee, maybe walk over Monday morning to see a new guy in jail. You could put Joel's file in the back of one of those file cabinets. It wouldn't be long before you forgot about it completely. Once you know something, you know it forever."

She was right. I'd already thought about all that during the slow walk from the car down the hill to the grave. I'd already decided against never knowing.

"I need to know."

She shrugged her shoulders underneath the big jacket and said, "Suit yourself." She walked around the grave a few steps and leaned against Danny's marble headstone. I stayed where I was. The girl was thin. She wasn't wearing traditional black, but instead a light blue dress hung below a heavy tan jacket. Her blonde hair was straight, and loose strands blew across the pale skin of her face. The blue eyes were deep and difficult, the concentration of her presence. Her hand reached up before she spoke and moved the hair from in front of her eyes.

Lisa said, "It wasn't Danny who was the crazy one, it was Joel. It wasn't my father, Emmitt Stabler, all torn up with mental illness, it's my mother. It runs in her family. My grandfather died in an institution. Momma's sister killed herself.

"My father did everything a man could do. He worked. He took care of us. He took care of my mother and put up with more than any person deserves. Do you have any idea what it's like being married to a schizophrenic? He was a saint. Daddy never laid a hand on any of us. There should be a shrine out here for my father instead of this."

She pointed to the headstone of Emmitt Stabler. It was smaller than Danny's stone, more weathered, harder to read. I found myself completely arrested by the story she told, not just the words, but the way she spoke them.

I didn't interrupt, but listened, and watched her mouth.

"Me and Danny never showed any signs, but Joel fought with it everyday. He was in and out of jail, he'd disappear for weeks at a time. There were rehabs, new medicines, self-medicating with alcohol or pills or whatever. He smoked cigarettes nonstop. Most of what I know, I know secondhand. My daddy got me out of that house when I was five. He sent me to live with my aunt and uncle. That's where I was raised.

"Danny wasn't so lucky. After I was sent away, and after Daddy died, Danny was left down here to carry the weight of my mother and my brother. I'm not sure who was heavier, but it was more than Danny could do. It was more than my father could do."

"Why would she lie?" I thought to myself. "What would be her motive?" Nothing. Not now. But some things didn't make sense. Lots of things. Could I have been manipulated to such a degree? It didn't seem possible. How much of what Joel told me was the truth? How much of what he said could I rely on? Maybe I didn't take enough time. Maybe one more session would have revealed everything. Was I used by Joel, or was I simply incapable of breaking through this one man's particular mental illness?

"I checked his criminal record," I said.

She smiled. "Let me guess, everything was in Danny's name? Joel used Danny's name when he got in trouble. He went so far as to get a driver's license in Danny's name one time. And of course, Danny wouldn't do anything about it. He was a lot like my father, too forgiving. That's what God's for, I think, to forgive folks. I'm not in the God business.

"And let me guess, every time you met with Joel he was wearing long sleeves, right? Because if he wasn't, you'd have seen all the lovely scars up and down his arms."

I saw the long sleeves clearly in my mind.

I asked, "If that's true, why would Danny let Joel, his mentally unbalanced brother, stand over him with a gun and basically execute him?"

Her expression didn't change. She wasn't trying to convince me of anything. Her words were full, but she didn't care whether I believed them or not.

"Joel wasn't standing over Danny, it was the other way around. If you read the autopsy report, Joel shot him in the head from below. The bullet had an upward angle. There was blood on the ceiling. It's still there. Why'd he shoot him? We'll never know. Even if Joel wasn't dead, we'd never know. Why did they both have guns? Why was Danny standing above Joel sitting on the couch? I've got my ideas of what happened, but it doesn't matter now, does it?"

My mind felt numb. She had an answer for everything. I looked over at the fresh black dirt. I should have walked away. I should have left the truth unturned.

The girl asked casually, "You didn't help him escape, did you?"

I looked up into those blue eyes and saw the little girl Joel had described. I could almost taste the sugar cookie they shared and feel the burn of the cold Coke on the back of my throat. I'd stepped over every line I'd ever drawn for myself, and I was afraid nothing would be the same again. Maybe I was glad nothing would be the same again.

"What about John Clayton?" I asked.

"I can remember my momma running through the house screaming how she was gonna leave us all and go live with John Clayton. I don't know how much was real and how much was in her head. Later on, after the man was dead, sometimes she'd still threaten to run off with him.

"But who knows, maybe he was Joel's father. Maybe my daddy's blood was strong enough to keep me and Danny in our right minds, but Joel wasn't so lucky. My momma used to go visit Preacher Clayton's grave all the time. It's right up the hill there."

She pointed, and I stared across the field of graves. The grayness of the day was constant. I found myself looking up into the mist and feeling the touch of tiny drops on my face. Inside my pocket, I touched my thumb to the underside of my wedding ring.

"Joel wasn't all bad," she said. "I remember when I was a little girl he'd come and wake me up in the morning. We'd sneak around the house and pretend."

With my face still to the sky I asked, "Did you eat sugar cookies and drink Cokes?"

I couldn't see it, but I know she smiled. I had my eyes closed, but I know the smile was genuine, and changed her face, like it changed mine.

Lisa said, "Yeah, we did. You never knew what he might do, good or bad, but I guess that's the nature of mental illness. Sometimes he was smart and funny, and sometimes he was scary. Sometimes he could be whoever he needed to be. He used to say it just depended on the seasons inside him. I don't really understand. I guess that's why my father sent me away, so I'd never understand. Now it's just me and Mom."

I lowered my eyes to see her and asked, "How do I know you're Lisa?"

She didn't smile. "You don't," she finally said.

"How do I know you're not the crazy one?" I asked.

"You don't," she said.

The girl walked past me and was gone from my sight. I didn't turn around. I didn't watch her walk up the hill, or get in a car, or drive away. I just stayed where I stood, all alone in the cemetery, and thought about the picture Joel drew of me. I stared at it for a long time that day. He saw me differently than I'd ever seen myself. I started to walk in the other direction, away from the car, up the hill.

What did I miss in him? What was hidden in the small pushes of his sentences, the subtleties of his questions, even the spacing of the pauses, the hollow moments in between? Had there been a connection, or just a purpose, and what was gained, and what was lost? Did nothing really matter, and was I then to recognize such a fact, and seek the certain road, and discover what I would discover?

I saw it in the drawings. I saw it in her eyes. I found myself finally at the grave of John Clayton, on the top of the hill, facing south, looking at the flowers at the base of the gray marble stone. They were fresh, the flowers, white and yellow like spring, in a small glass jar.

I stood and waited for something, but there was nothing. I finally turned to leave, but my eye was caught. On top of the headstone, resting in the center, I saw something. A penny. A shiny copper penny, alone, placed perfectly above the name of John Clayton.

I stopped in mid-step, my body turned to leave, my head the other way, one step from seeing heads or tails. One decision away from knowing my future, good luck or bad.

ACKNOWLEDGMENTS

In my prior books I have acknowledged friends, family, and people who have helped me in the writing world and elsewhere. It is high time I recognized David Poindexter appropriately. He is the only publisher I have ever known, and God-willing, my publisher for life. I do not believe I have ever met a man of such unsurrendering faith. He believes completely in the goodness and potential of the written word, and maintains this faith in the riptide of an industry full of non-believers. Thank you, David.